Adventures of the Pugulatmu'j
VOL. 1

GIJU'S GIFT

Brandon Mitchell   Veronika Barinova

HIGHWATER
PRESS

Canada Council   Conseil des arts
for the Arts   du Canada

We acknowledge the support of the Canada Council for the Arts.
Nous remercions le Conseil des arts du Canada de son soutien.

HighWater Press gratefully acknowledges the financial support of the
Province of Manitoba through the Department of Sport, Culture and Heritage
and the Manitoba Book Publishing Tax Credit, and the Government of Canada
through the Canada Book Fund (CBF), for our publishing activities.

HighWater Press is an imprint of Portage & Main Press.
Printed and bound in Canada by Friesens
Design by Jennifer Lum
Concept sketches for characters and for page 45 by Brandon Mitchell
Lettering by Britt Wilson

Library and Archives Canada Cataloguing in Publication
Title: Giju's gift / Brandon Mitchell, Veronika Barinova. Names: Mitchell, Brandon, author.
Barinova, Veronika, artist. Description: Series statement: Adventures of the Pugulatmu'j ; 1
Identifiers: Canadiana (print) 20210347066 | Canadiana (ebook) 20210347082 | ISBN 9781553799474
(softcover) | ISBN 9781553799481 (EPUB) | ISBN 9781553799498 (PDF) Subjects: LCGFT: Graphic novels.
Classification: LCC PN6733.M58 G55 2022 | DDC j741.5/971—dc23

25 24 23 22   1 2 3 4 5

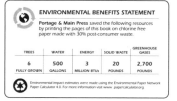

ENVIRONMENTAL BENEFITS STATEMENT

Portage & Main Press saved the following resources
by printing the pages of this book on chlorine free
paper made with 30% post-consumer waste.

TREES	WATER	ENERGY	SOLID WASTE	GREENHOUSE GASES
6 FULLY GROWN	500 GALLONS	3 MILLION BTUs	20 POUNDS	2,700 POUNDS

Environmental impact estimates were made using the Environmental Paper Network
Paper Calculator 4.0. For more information visit www.papercalculator.org

FSC
www.fsc.org
MIX
Paper from
responsible sources
FSC® C016245

HIGHWATER
PRESS
www.highwaterpress.com
Winnipeg, Manitoba
Treaty 1 Territory and homeland of the Métis Nation

This story would not be possible without the support
of my loving wife, Natasha Martin-Mitchell,
and my sons, Brayden and Bryce,
who keep me motivated to keep creating.

—BM

For Oxana,
who has always supported my creative side
and motivated me to make art.

—VB

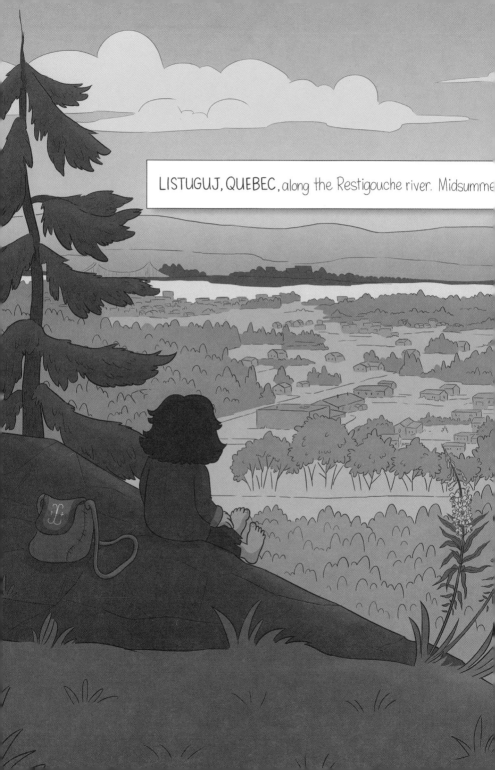

LISTUGUJ, QUEBEC, along the Restigouche river. Midsumme

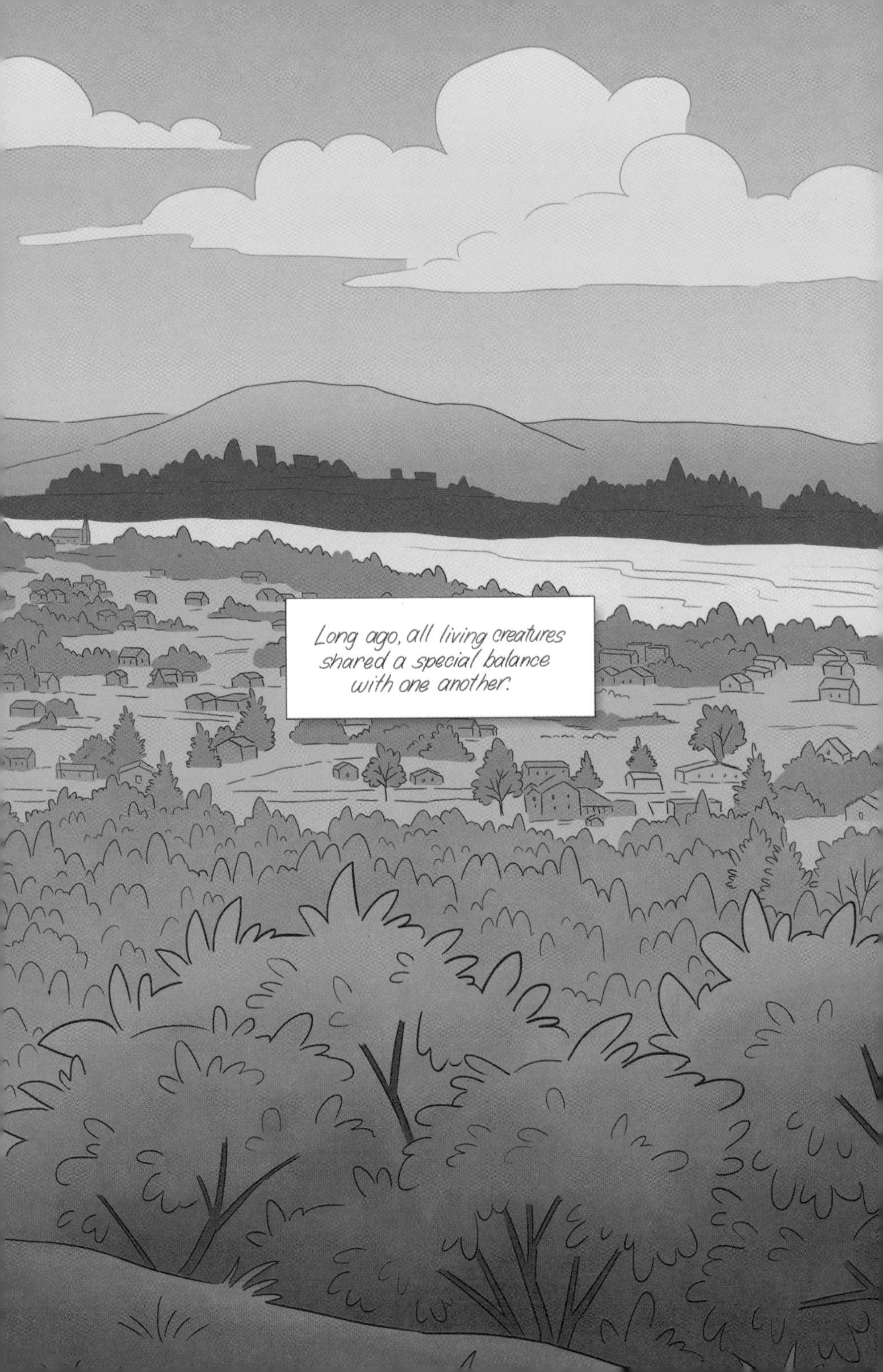
Long ago, all living creatures shared a special balance with one another.

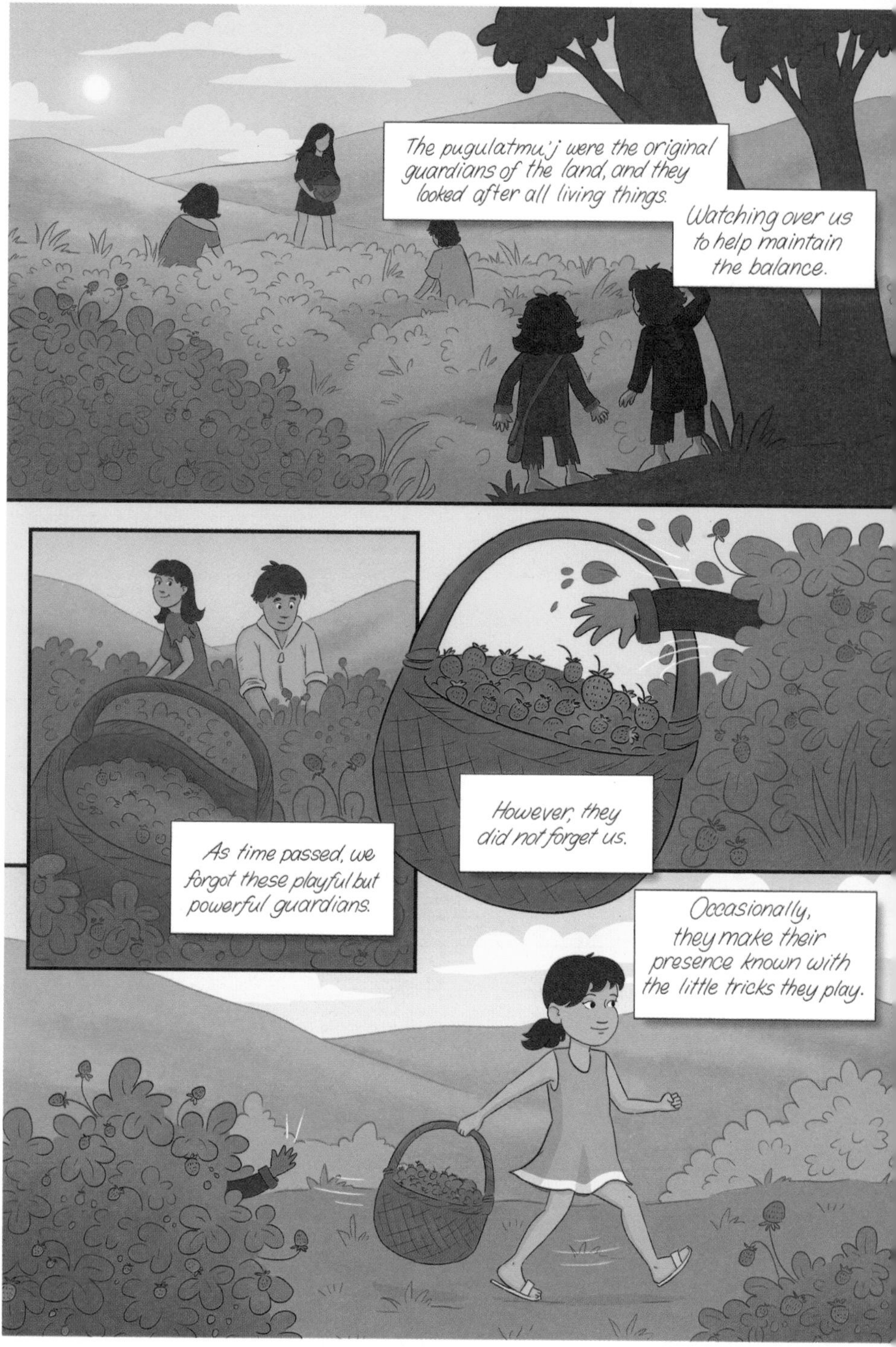
The pugulatmu'j were the original guardians of the land, and they looked after all living things.
Watching over us to help maintain the balance.
As time passed, we forgot these playful but powerful guardians.
However, they did not forget us.
Occasionally, they make their presence known with the little tricks they play.

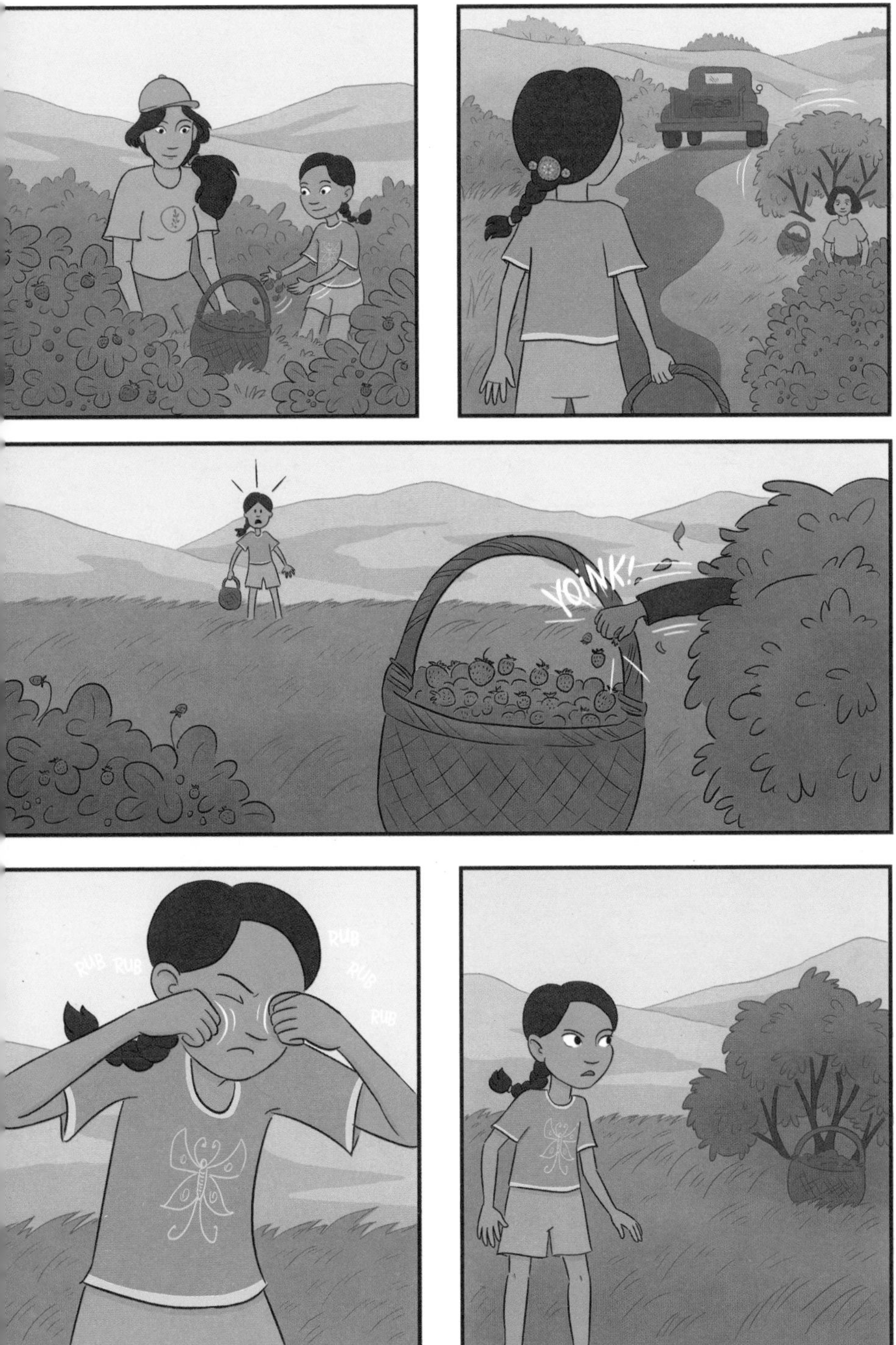
YOINK!
RUB RUB
RUB
RUB
RUB

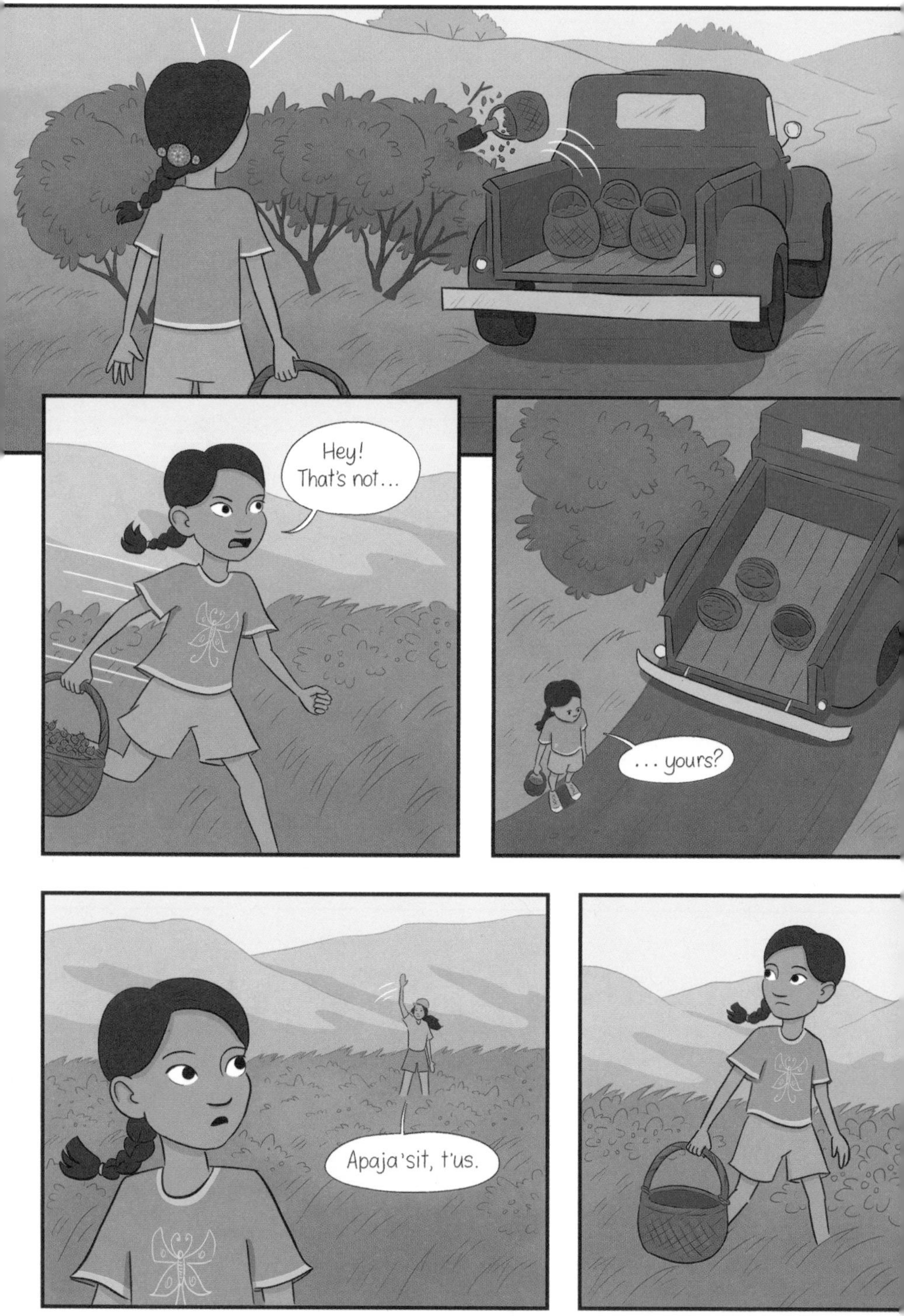
Hey!
That's not...
... yours?
Apaja'sit, t'us.

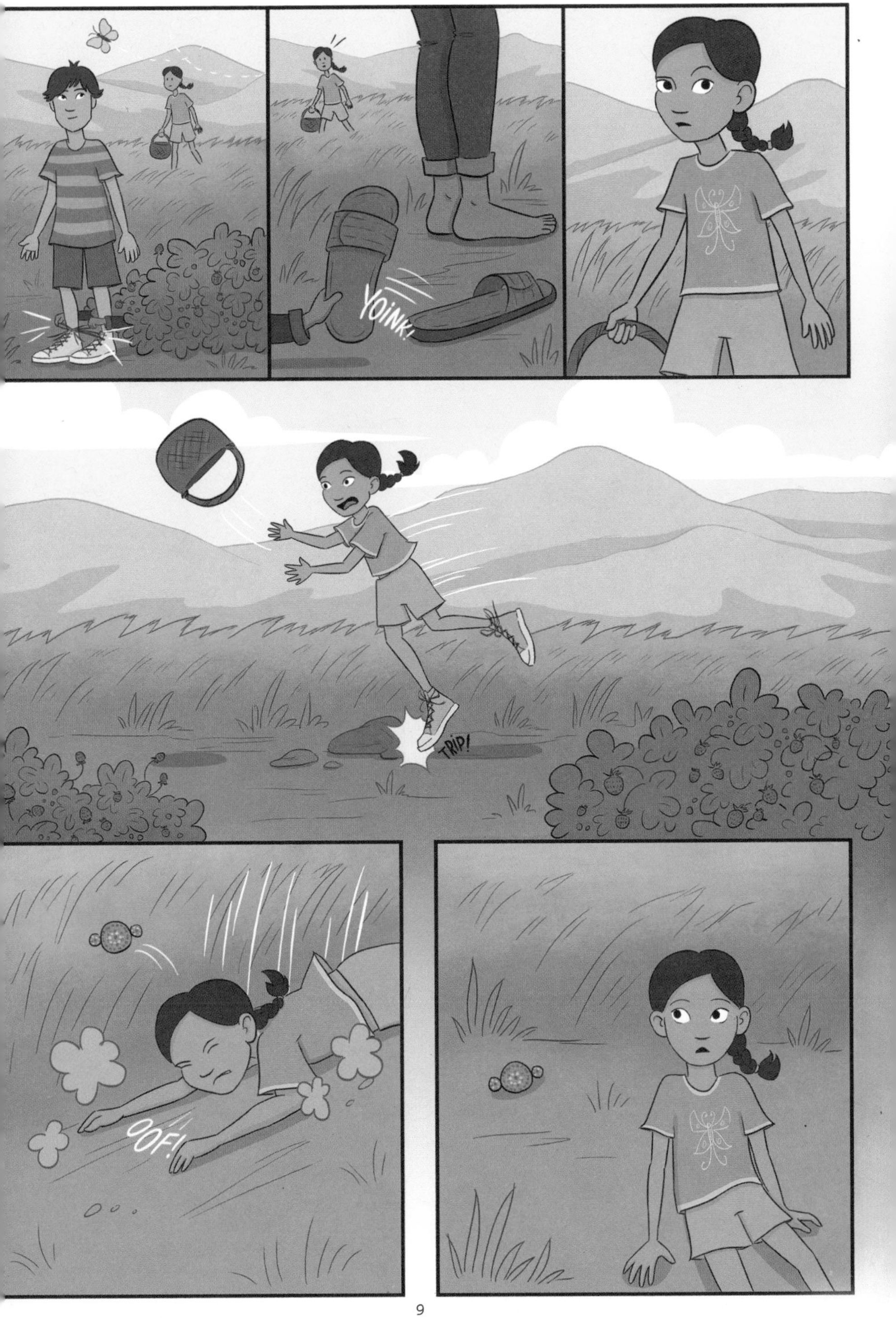
YOINK!
TRIP!
OOF!

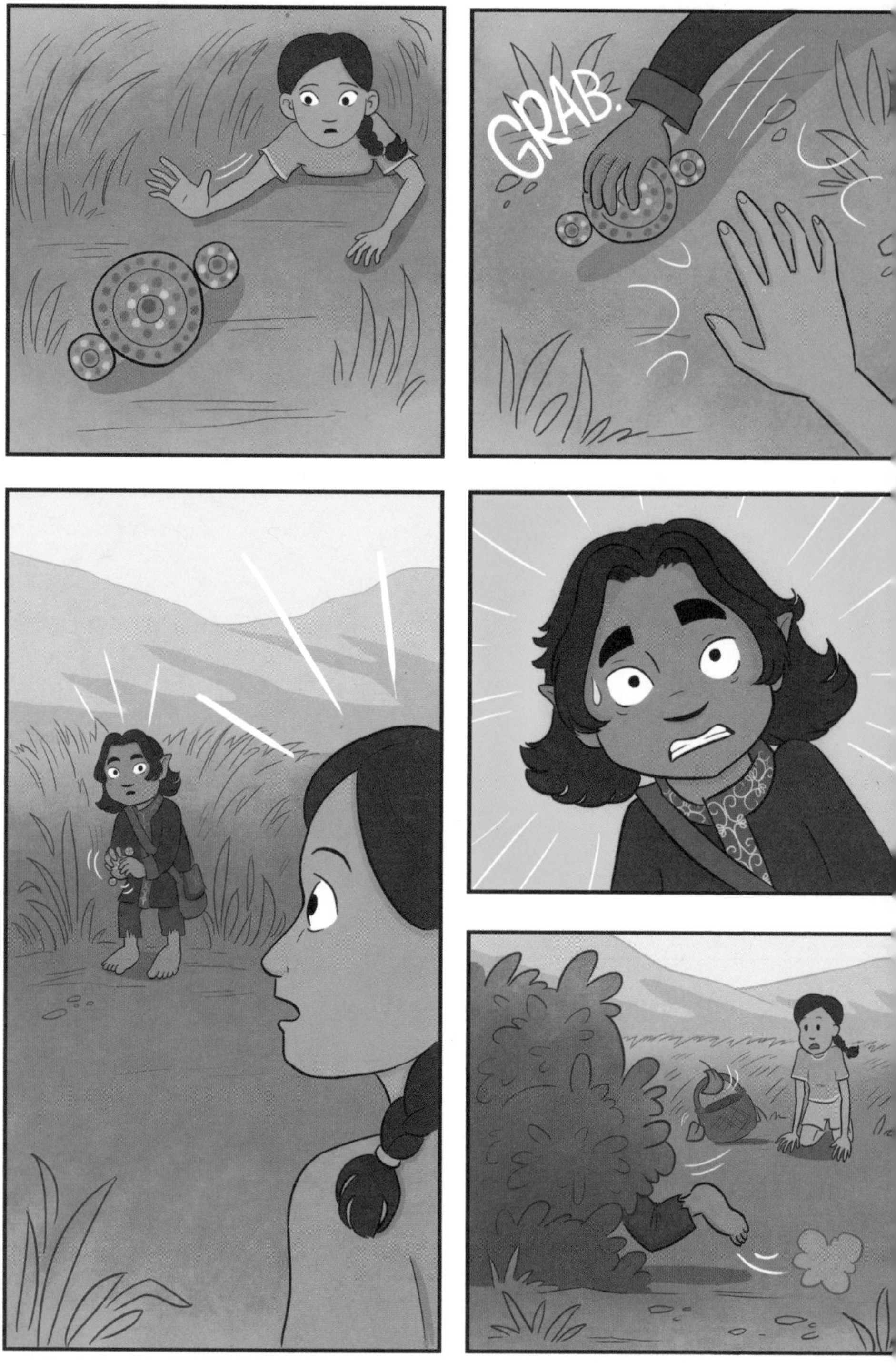
GRAB.

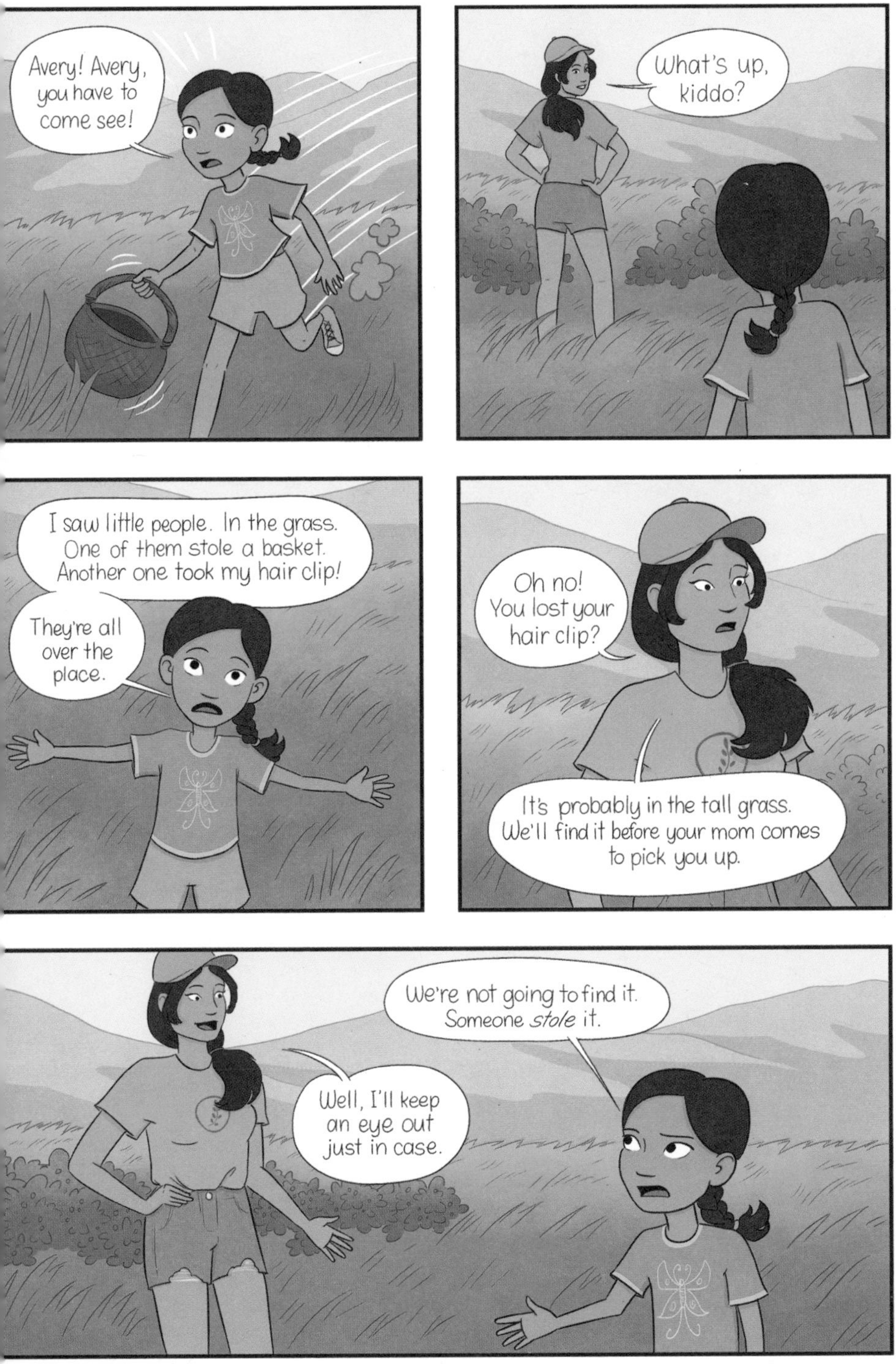
Avery! Avery, you have to come see!
What's up, kiddo?
I saw little people. In the grass. One of them stole a basket. Another one took my hair clip!
They're all over the place.
Oh no! You lost your hair clip?
It's probably in the tall grass. We'll find it before your mom comes to pick you up.
We're not going to find it. Someone *stole* it.
Well, I'll keep an eye out just in case.

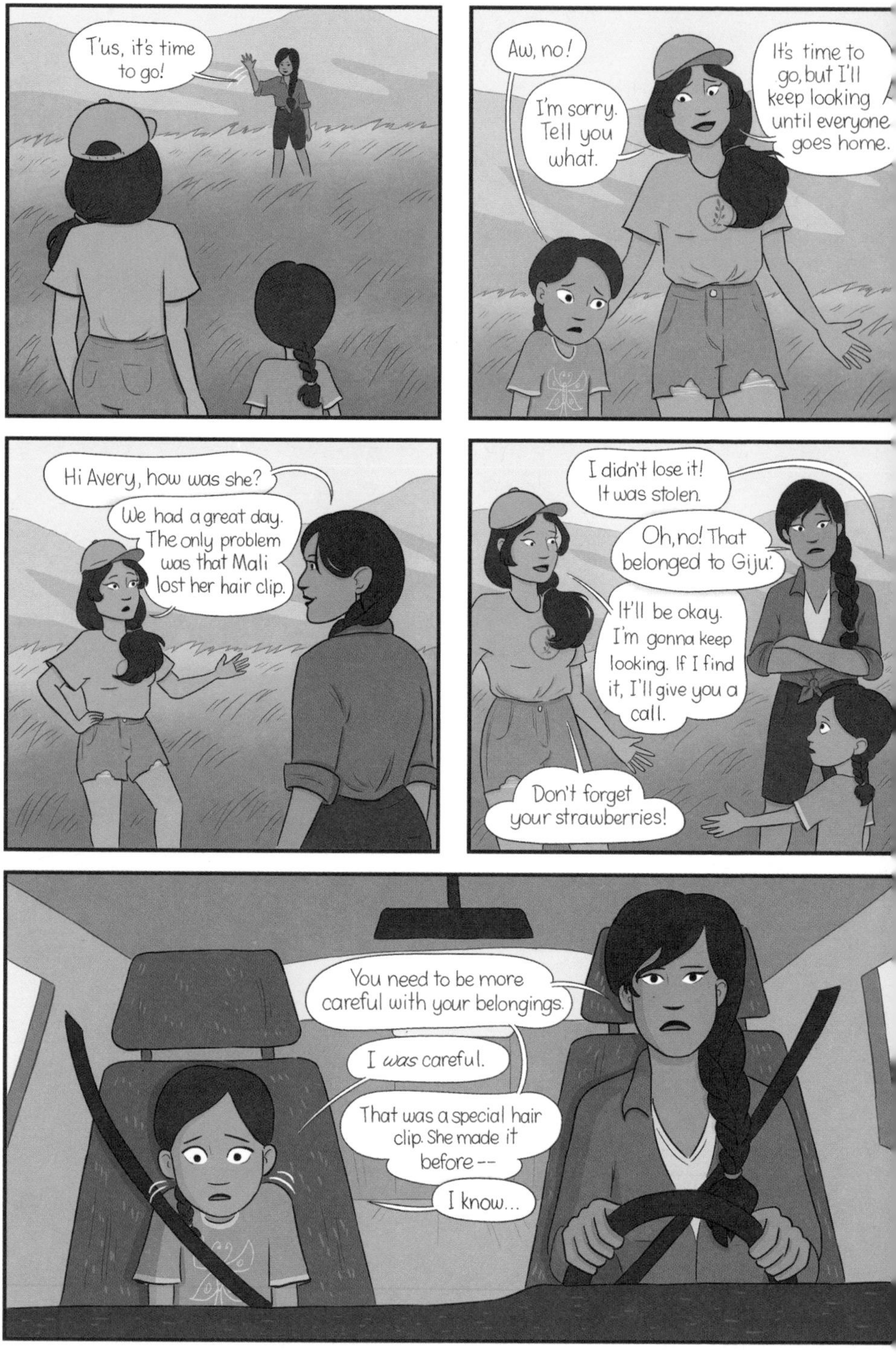
T'us, it's time to go!
Aw, no!
I'm sorry. Tell you what.
It's time to go, but I'll keep looking until everyone goes home.
Hi Avery, how was she?
We had a great day. The only problem was that Mali lost her hair clip.
I didn't lose it! It was stolen.
Oh, no! That belonged to Giju'.
It'll be okay. I'm gonna keep looking. If I find it, I'll give you a call.
Don't forget your strawberries!
You need to be more careful with your belongings.
I *was* careful.
That was a special hair clip. She made it before --
I know...

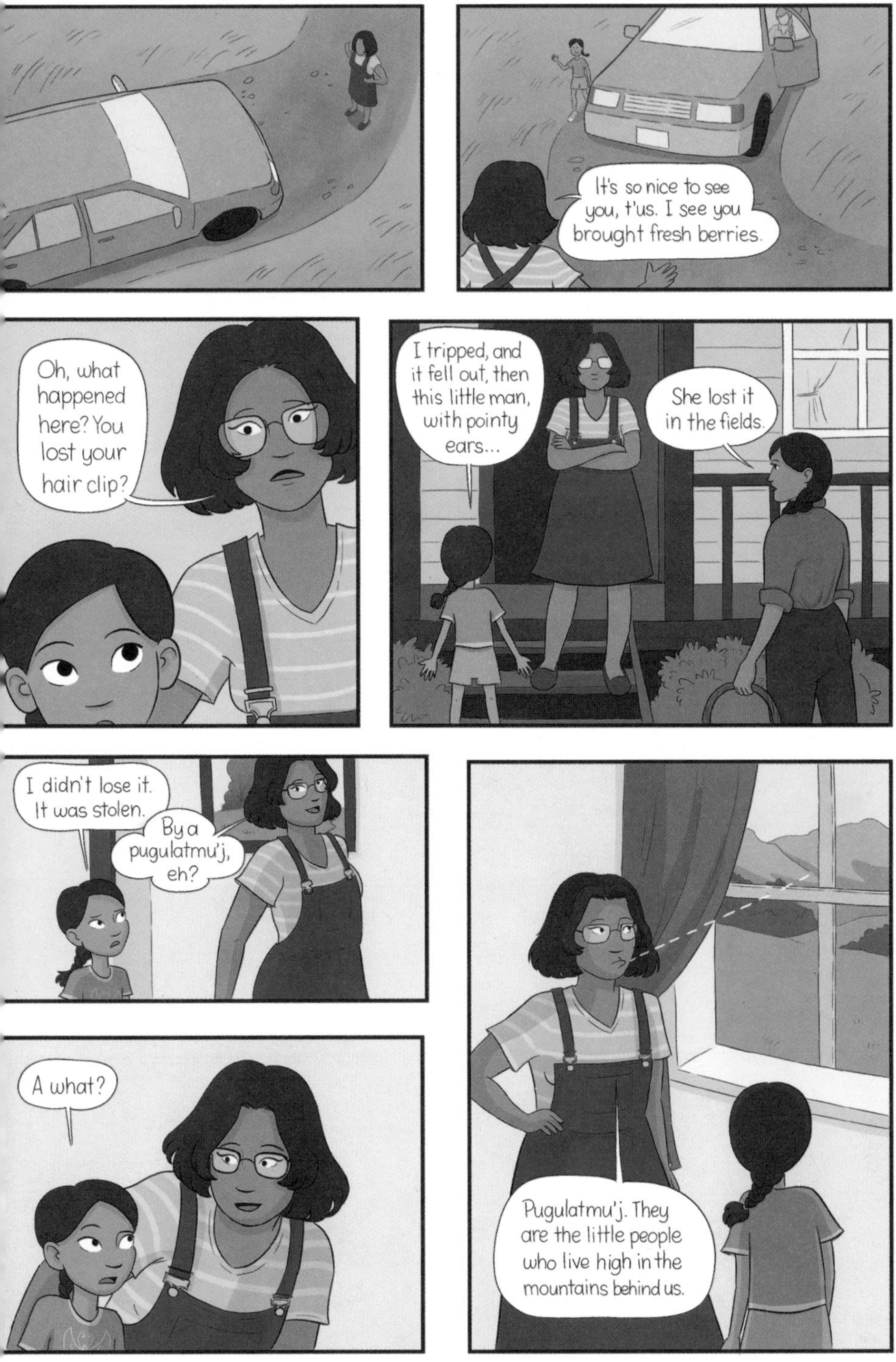

It's so nice to see you, t'us. I see you brought fresh berries.
Oh, what happened here? You lost your hair clip?
I tripped, and it fell out, then this little man, with pointy ears...
She lost it in the fields.
I didn't lose it. It was stolen.
By a pugulatmu'j, eh?
A what?
Pugulatmu'j. They are the little people who live high in the mountains behind us.

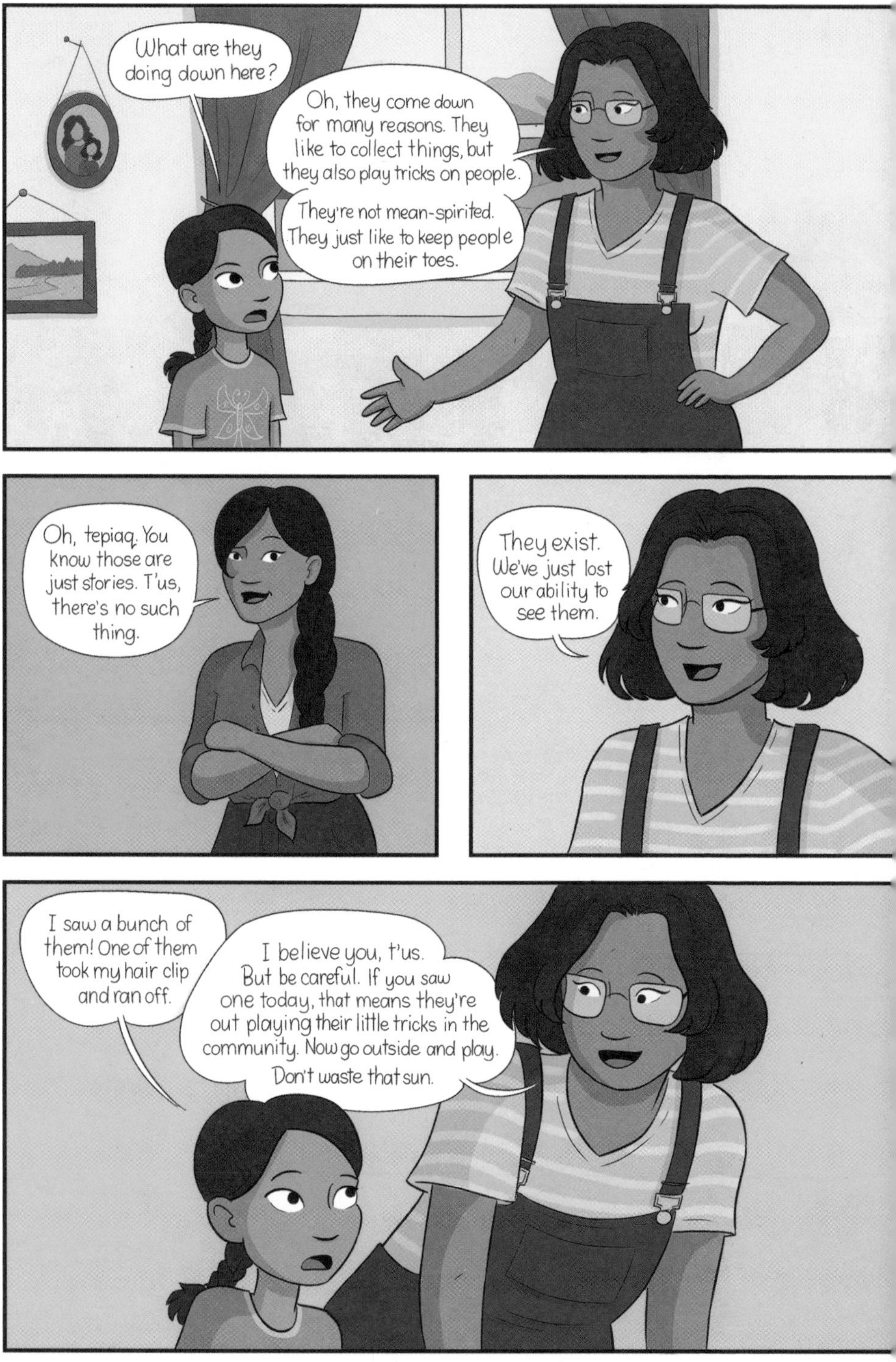
What are they doing down here?
Oh, they come down for many reasons. They like to collect things, but they also play tricks on people.
They're not mean-spirited. They just like to keep people on their toes.
Oh, tepiaq. You know those are just stories. T'us, there's no such thing.
They exist. We've just lost our ability to see them.
I saw a bunch of them! One of them took my hair clip and ran off.
I believe you, t'us. But be careful. If you saw one today, that means they're out playing their little tricks in the community. Now go outside and play.
Don't waste that sun.

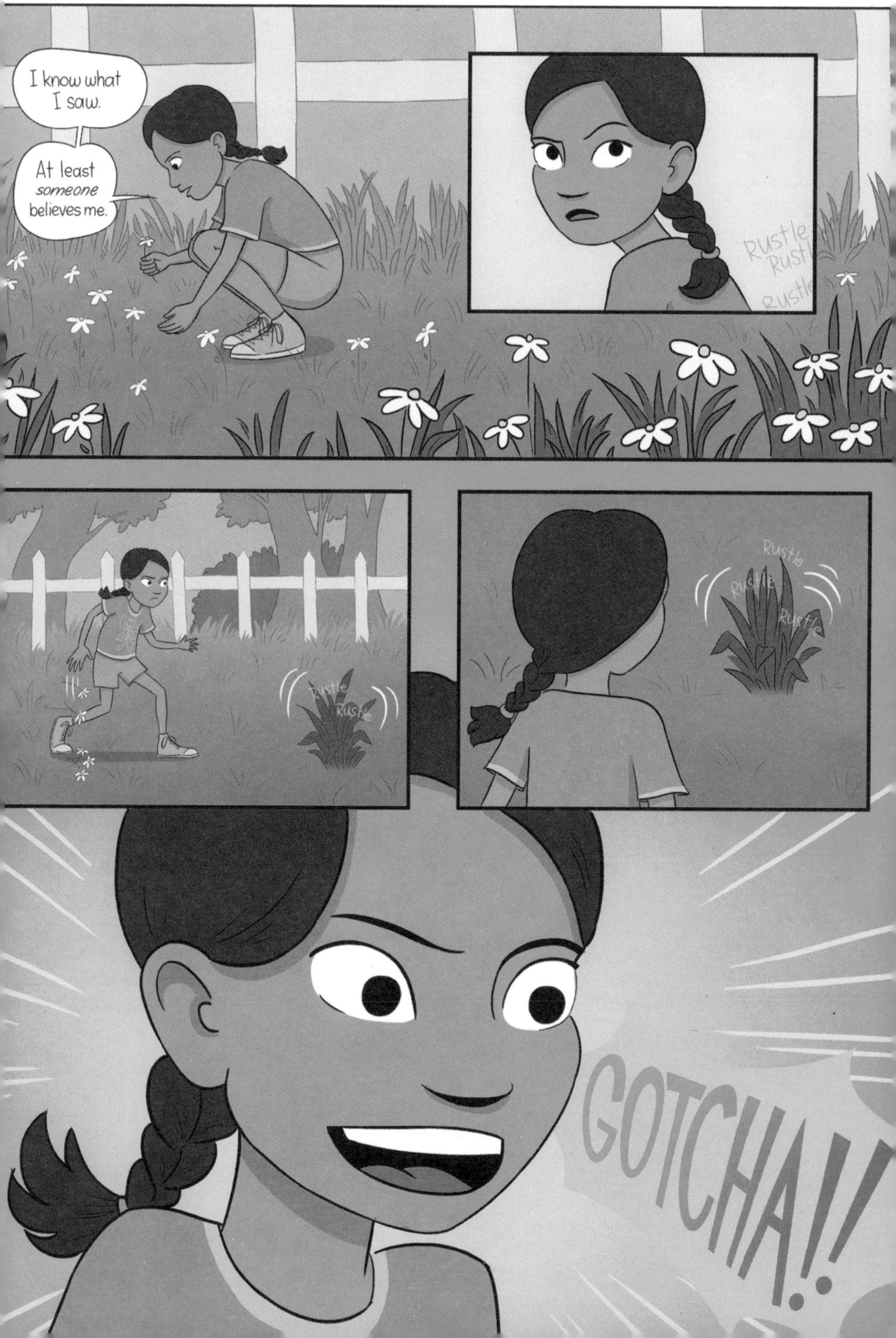
I know what I saw.
At least *someone* believes me.
Rustle Rustle Rustle
Rustle Rustle
Rustle Rustle Rustle
GOTCHA!!

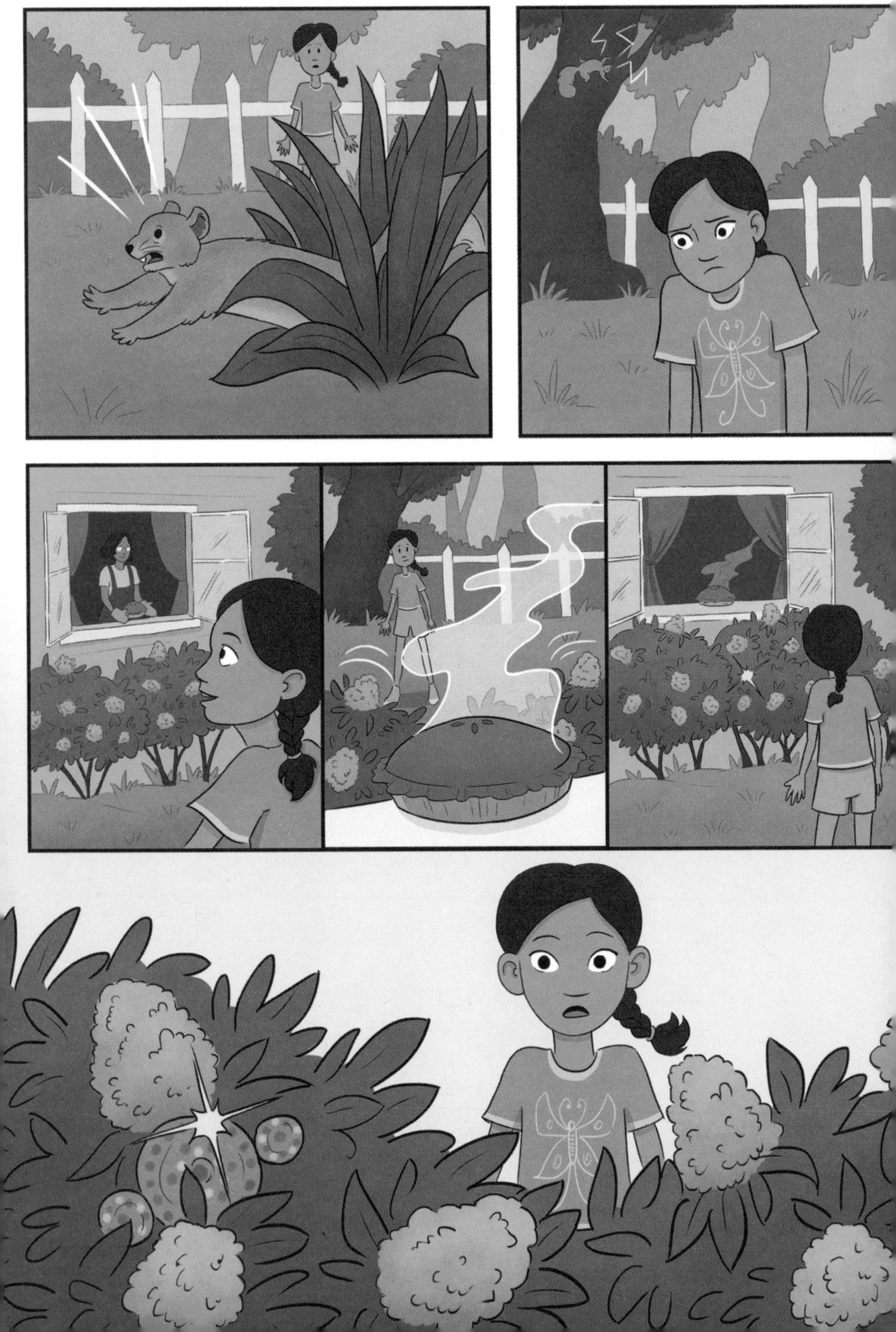

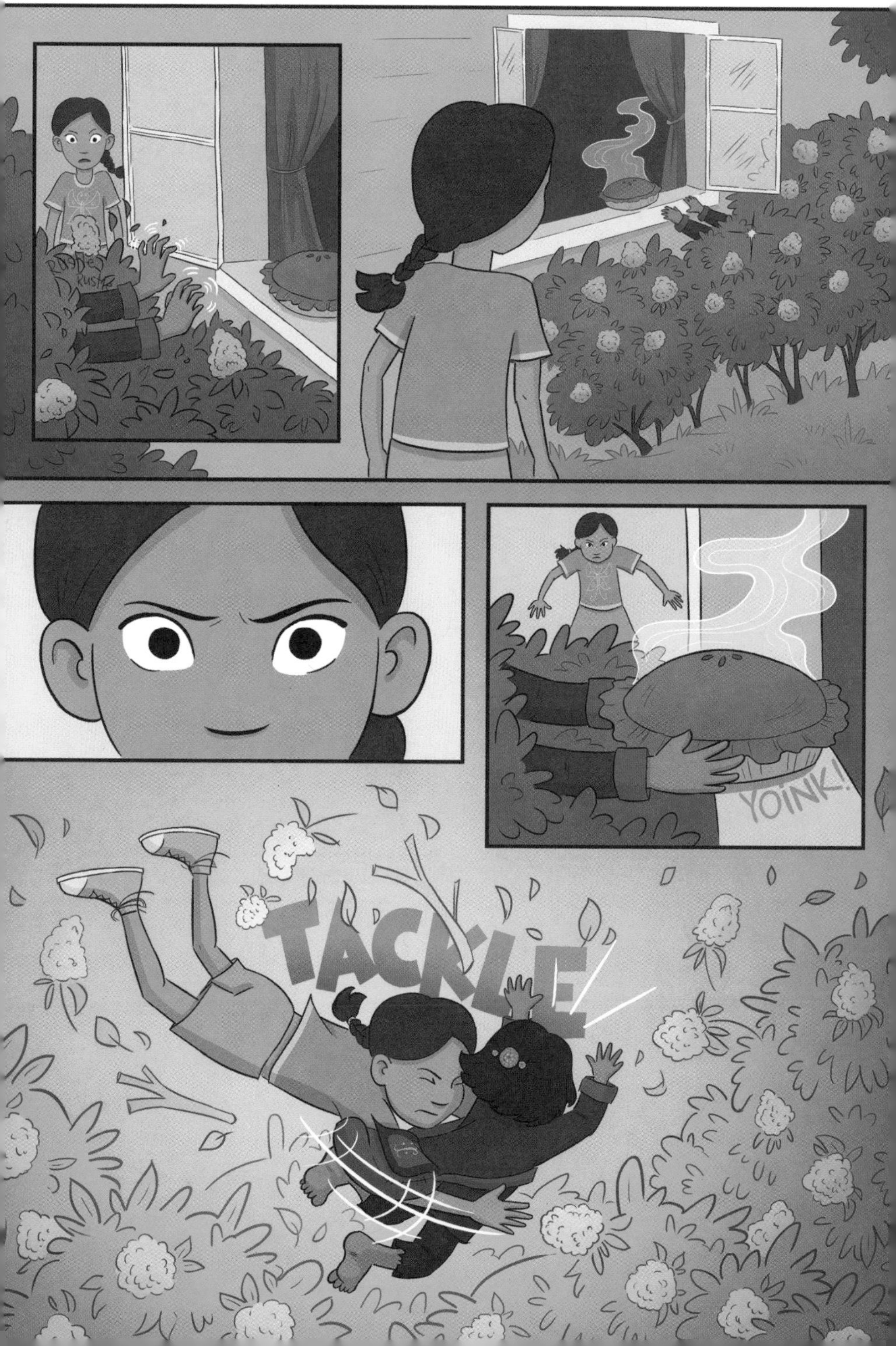
YOINK!
TACKLE

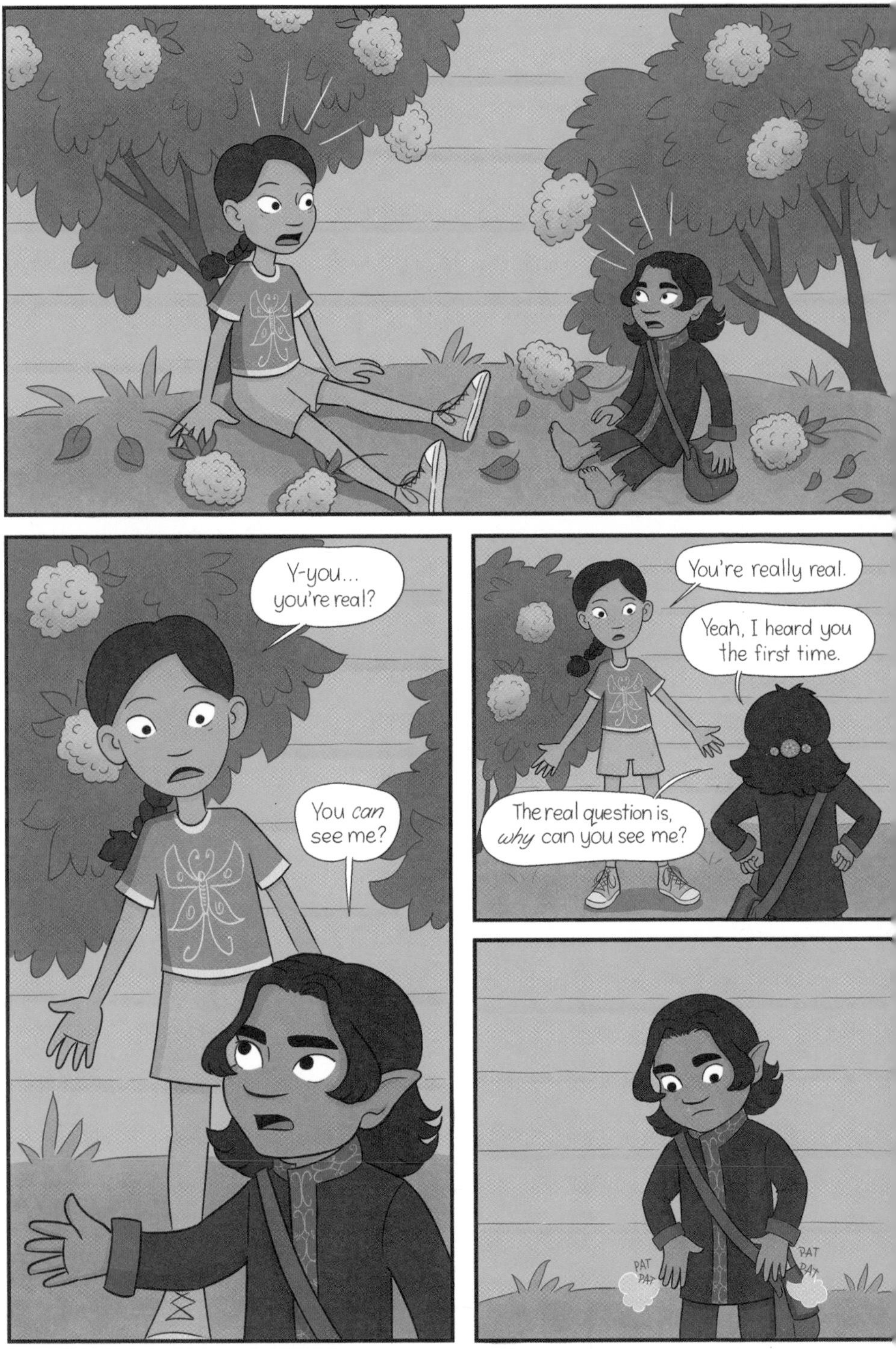
Y-you... you're real?
You *can* see me?
You're really real.
Yeah, I heard you the first time.
The real question is, *why* can you see me?
PAT PAT
PAT PAT

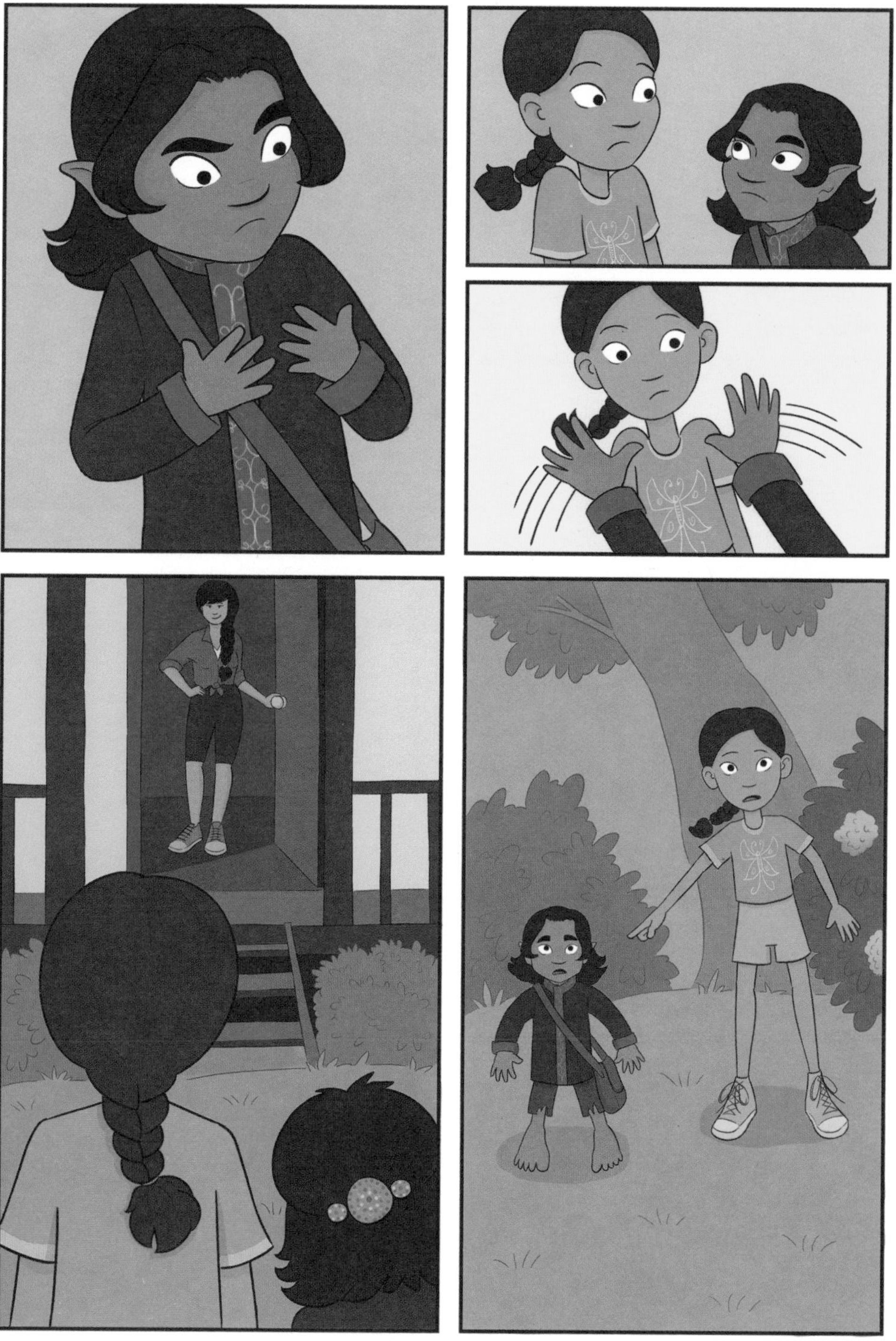

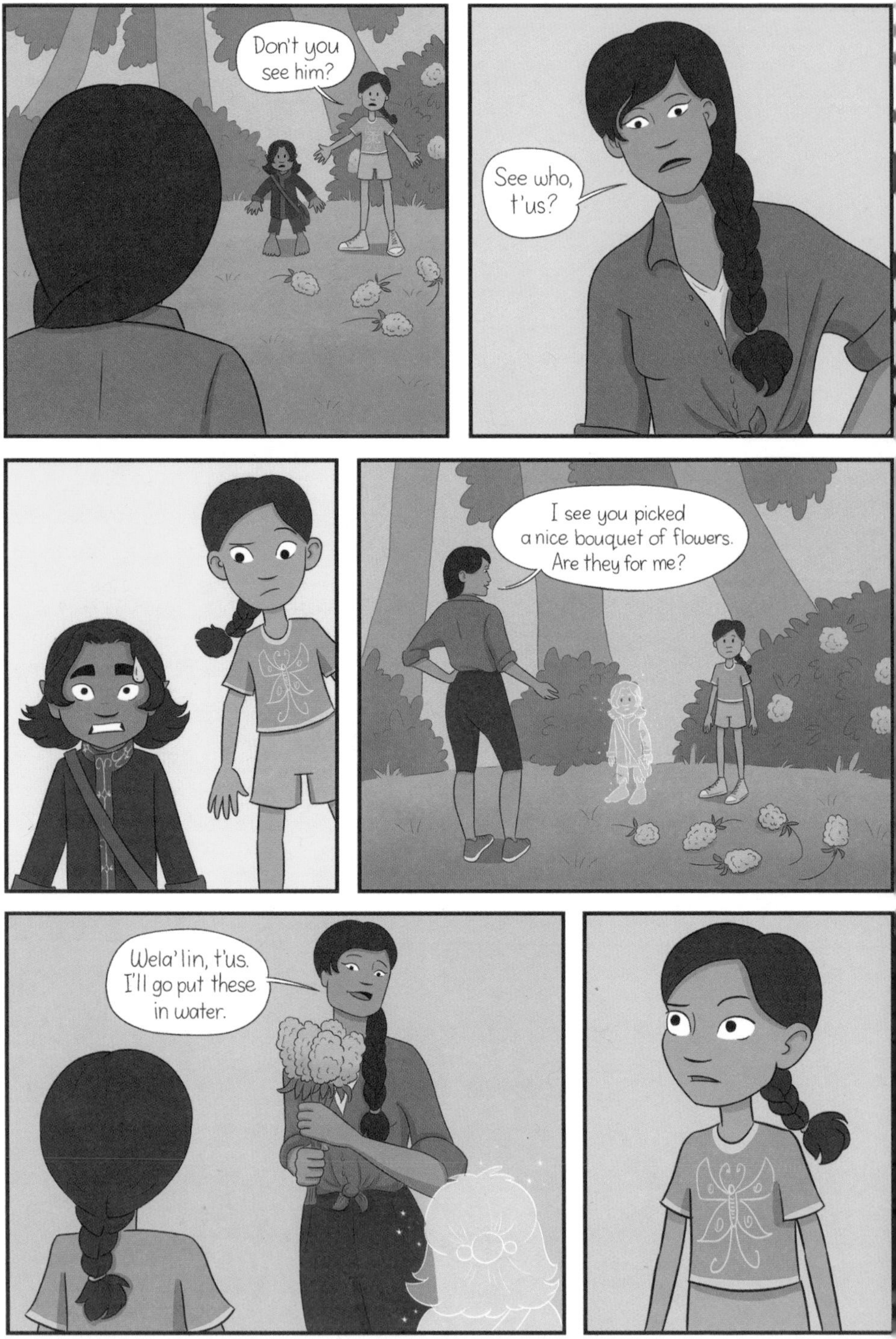
Don't you see him?
See who, t'us?
I see you picked a nice bouquet of flowers. Are they for me?
Wela'lin, t'us. I'll go put these in water.

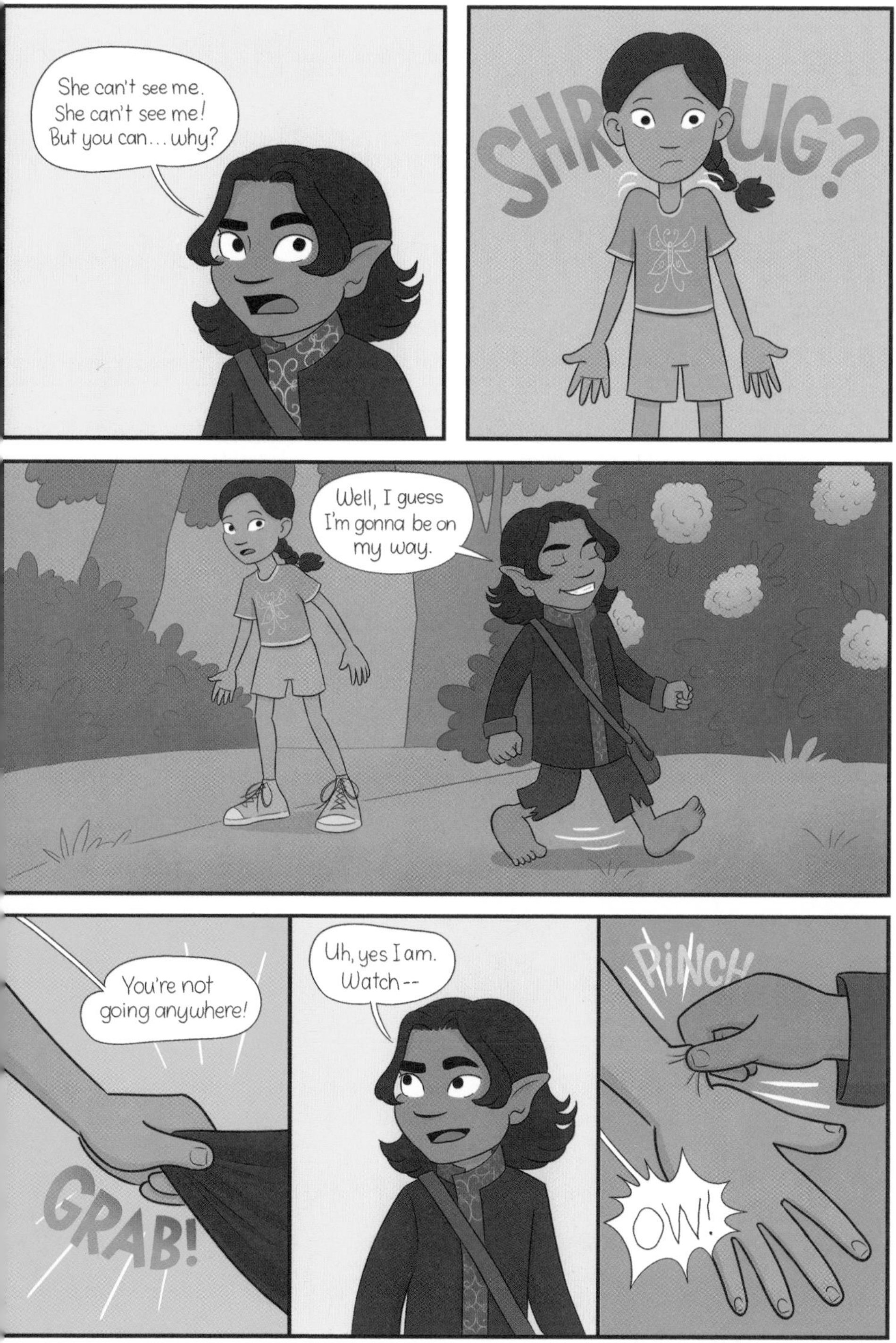
She can't see me.
She can't see me!
But you can... why?
SHRUG?
Well, I guess
I'm gonna be on
my way.
You're not
going anywhere!
GRAB!
Uh, yes I am.
Watch--
PINCH
OW!

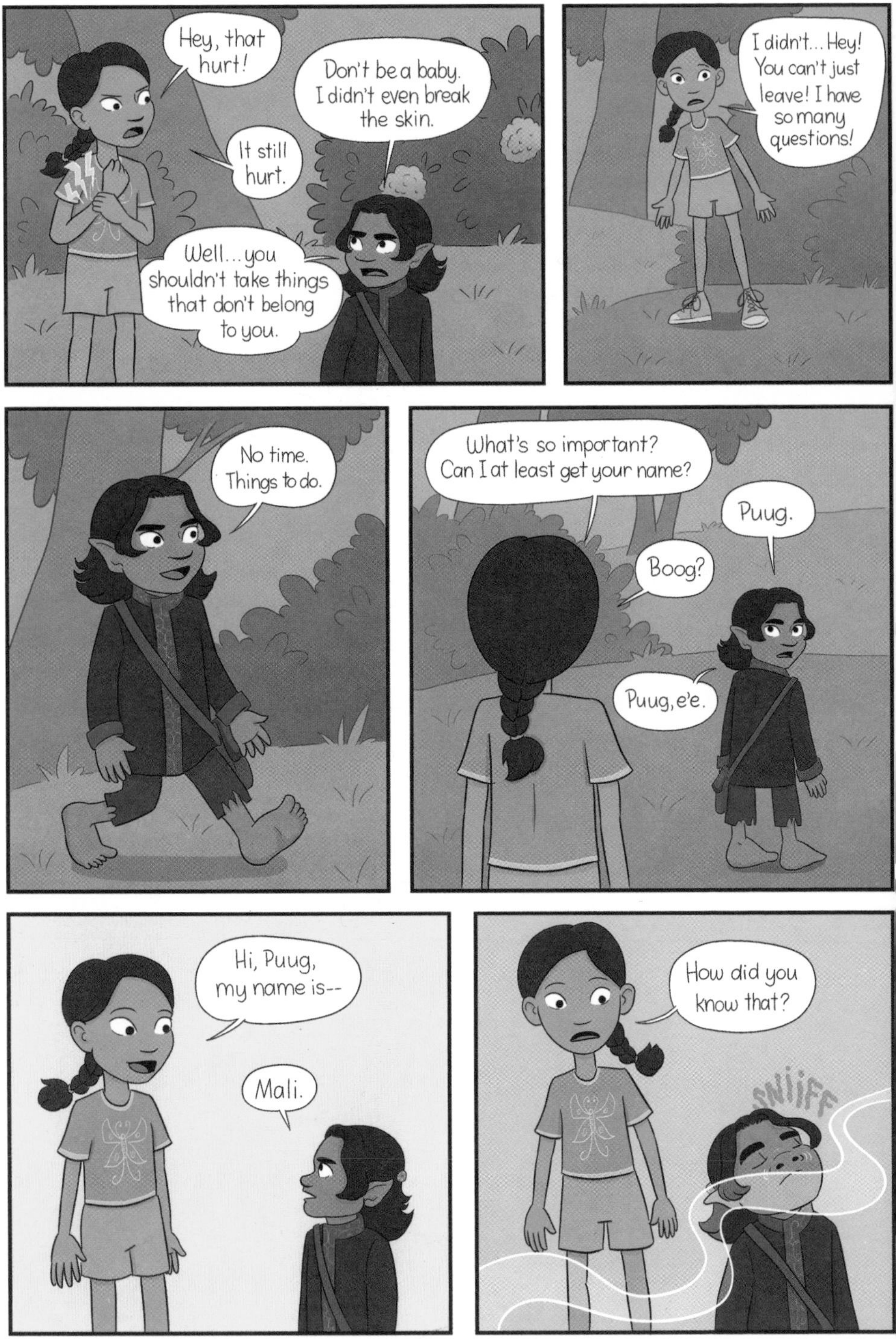
Hey, that hurt!
Don't be a baby. I didn't even break the skin.
It still hurt.
Well... you shouldn't take things that don't belong to you.
I didn't... Hey! You can't just leave! I have so many questions!
No time. Things to do.
What's so important? Can I at least get your name?
Puug.
Boog?
Puug, e'e.
Hi, Puug, my name is--
Mali.
How did you know that?
SNIIFF

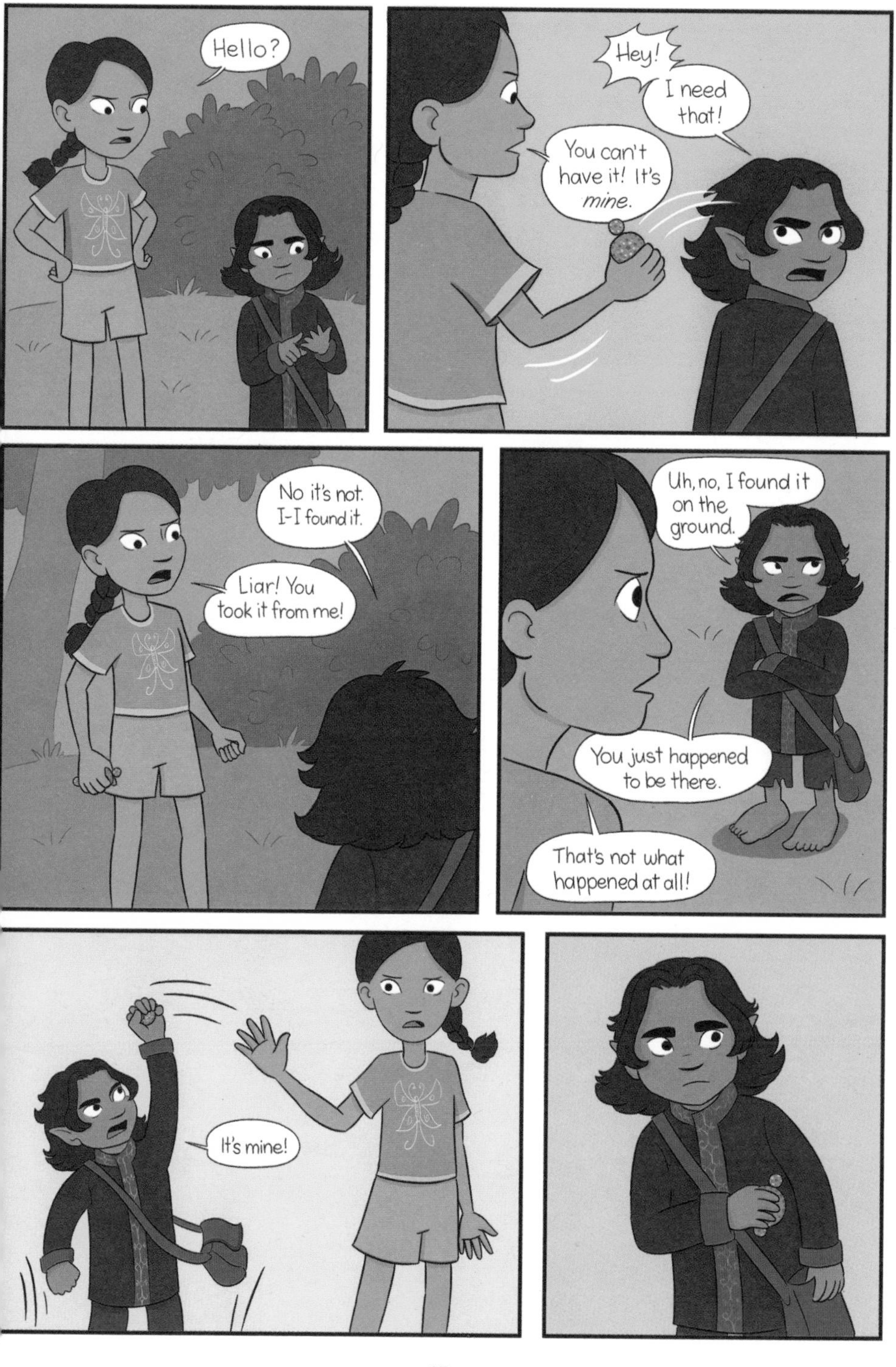
Hello?
Hey!
I need that!
You can't have it! It's *mine*.
No it's not. I-I found it.
Liar! You took it from me!
Uh, no, I found it on the ground.
You just happened to be there.
That's not what happened at all!
It's mine!

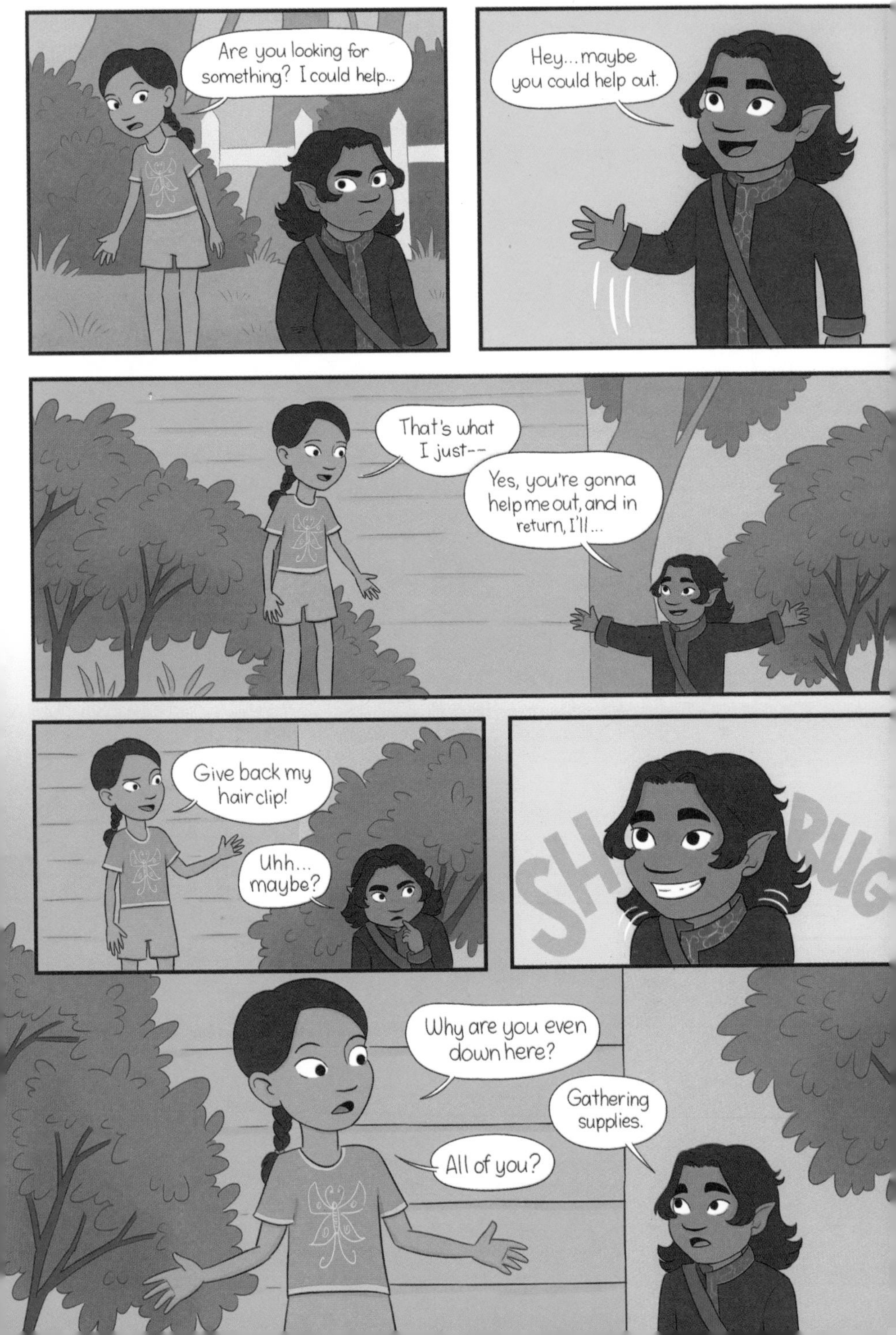
Are you looking for something? I could help...
Hey... maybe you could help out.
That's what I just--
Yes, you're gonna help me out, and in return, I'll...
Give back my hair clip!
Uhh... maybe?
SHRUG
Why are you even down here?
Gathering supplies.
All of you?

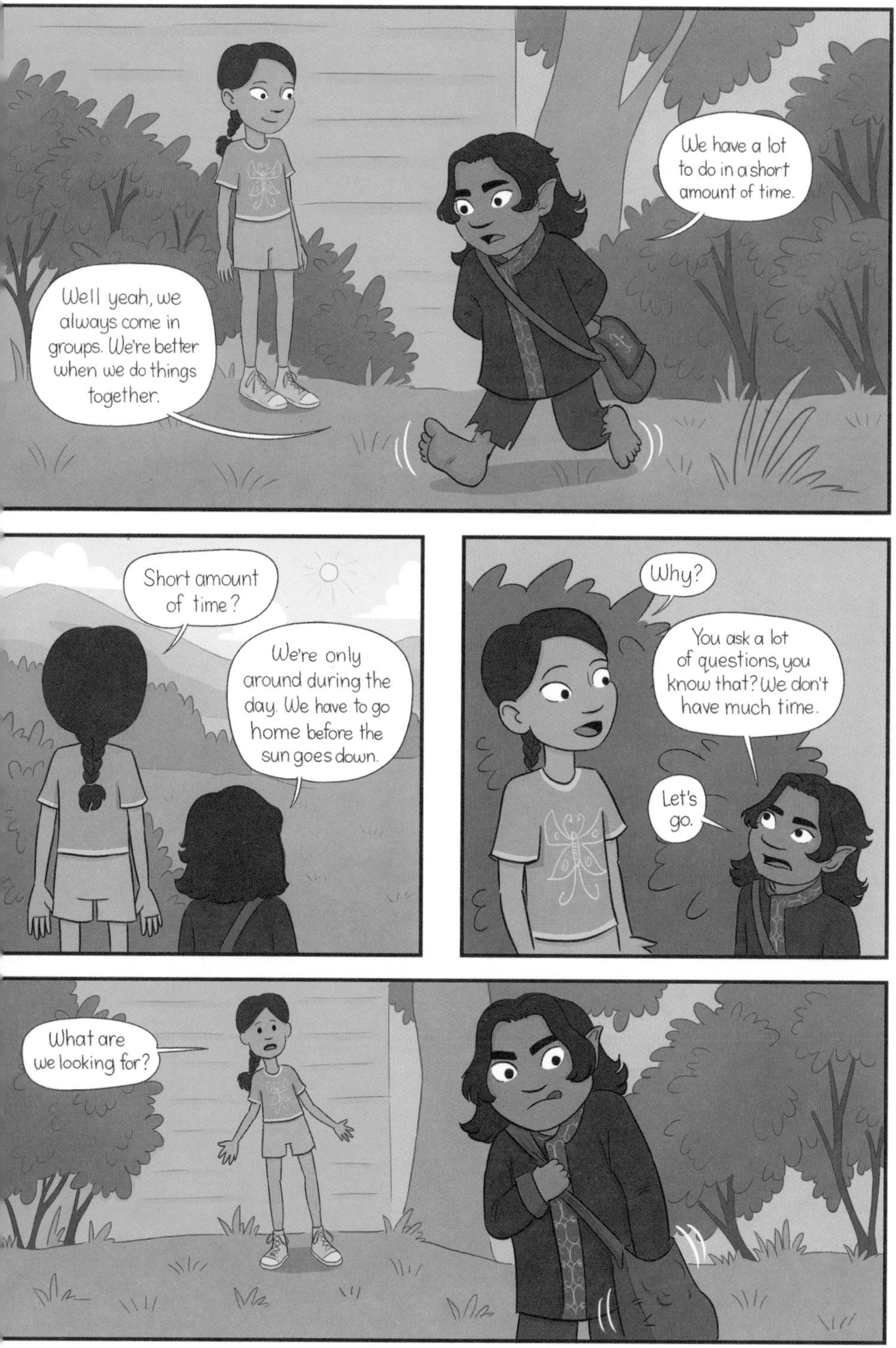
We have a lot to do in a short amount of time.
Well yeah, we always come in groups. We're better when we do things together.
Short amount of time?
We're only around during the day. We have to go home before the sun goes down.
Why?
You ask a lot of questions, you know that? We don't have much time.
Let's go.
What are we looking for?

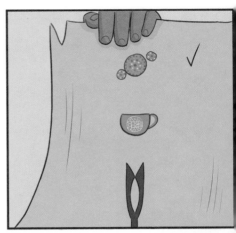

Why do you need a teacup?

It's important--

But you won't tell me.

Right.

Fine.

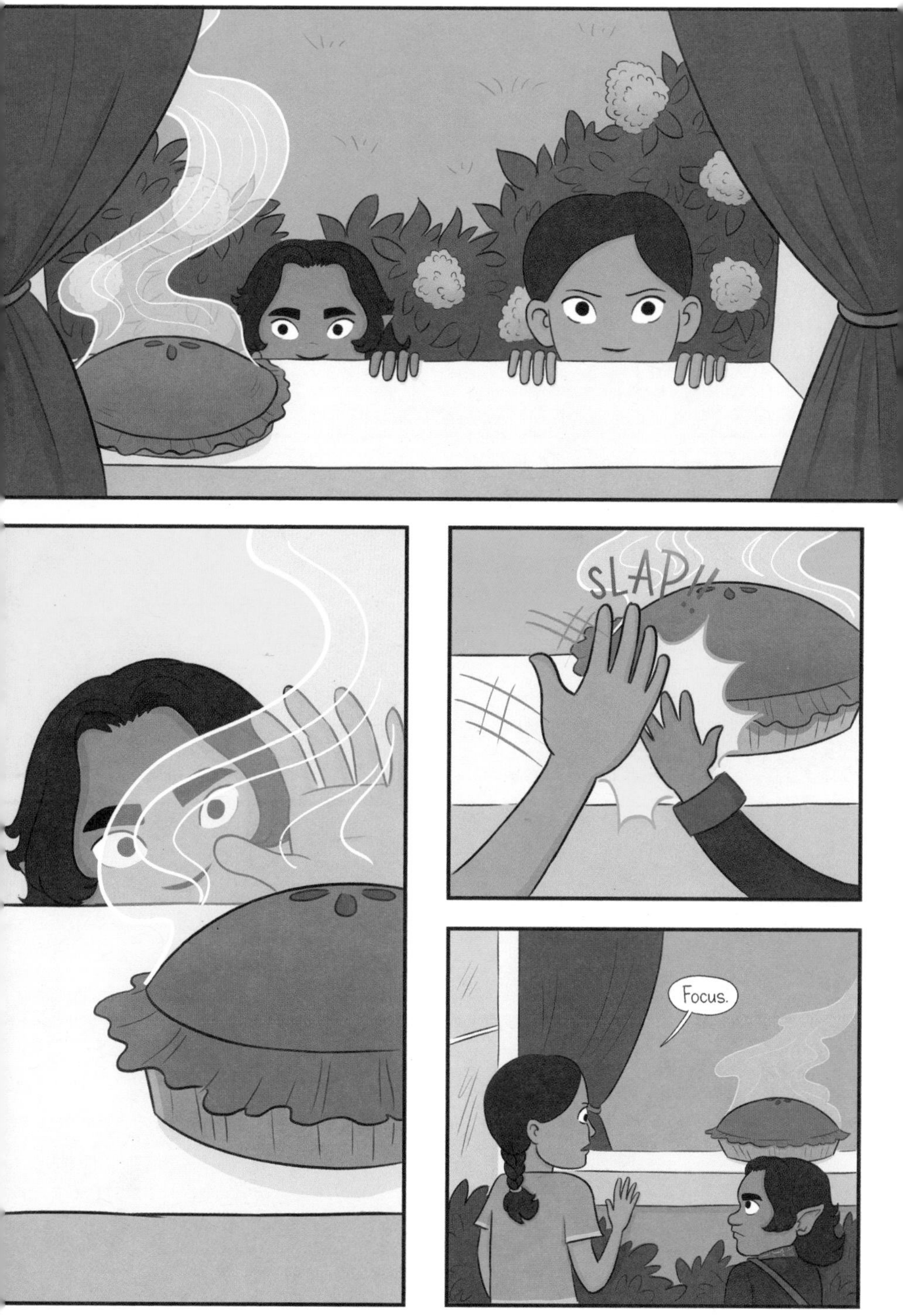
SLAP!!
Focus.

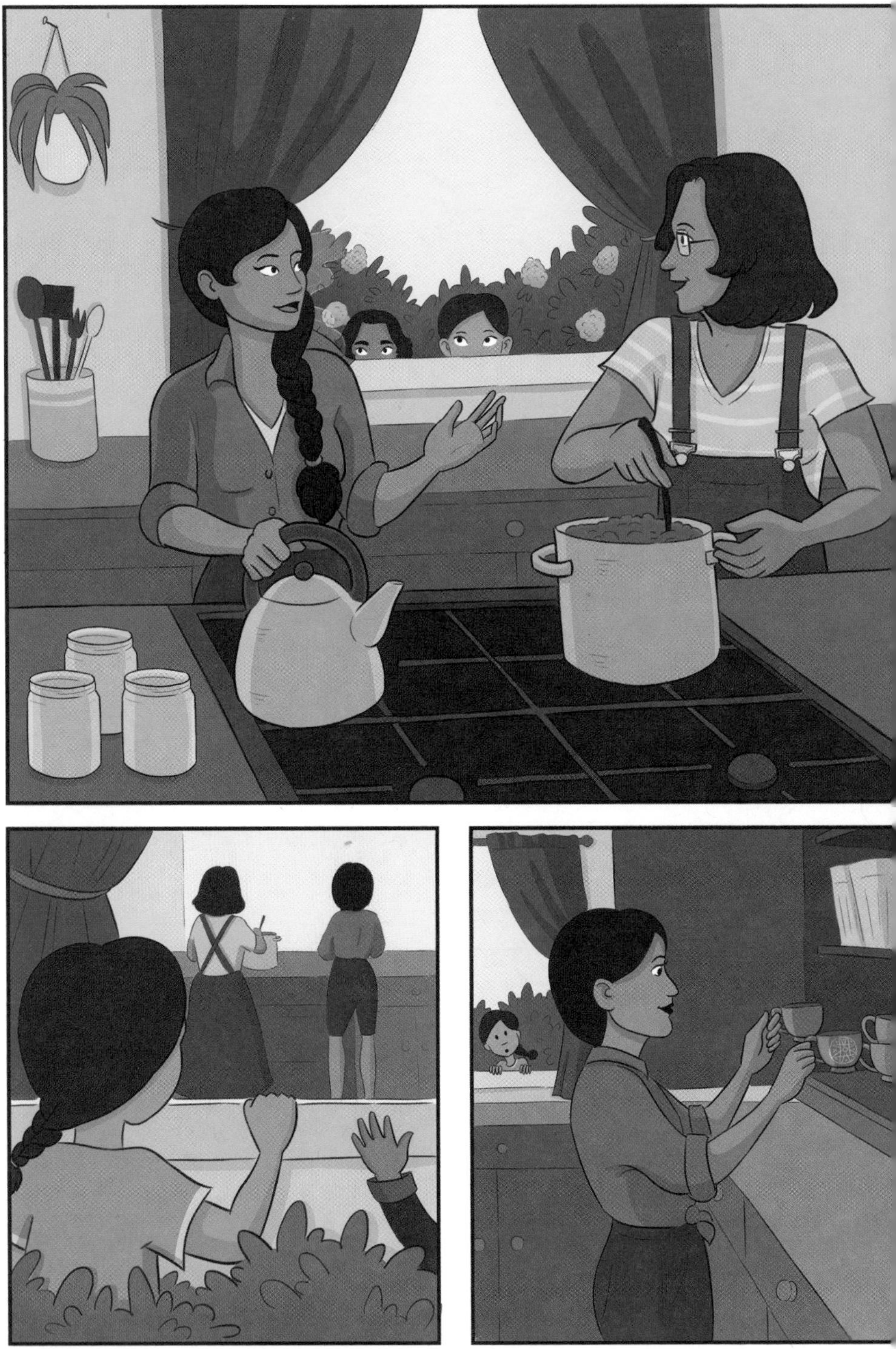

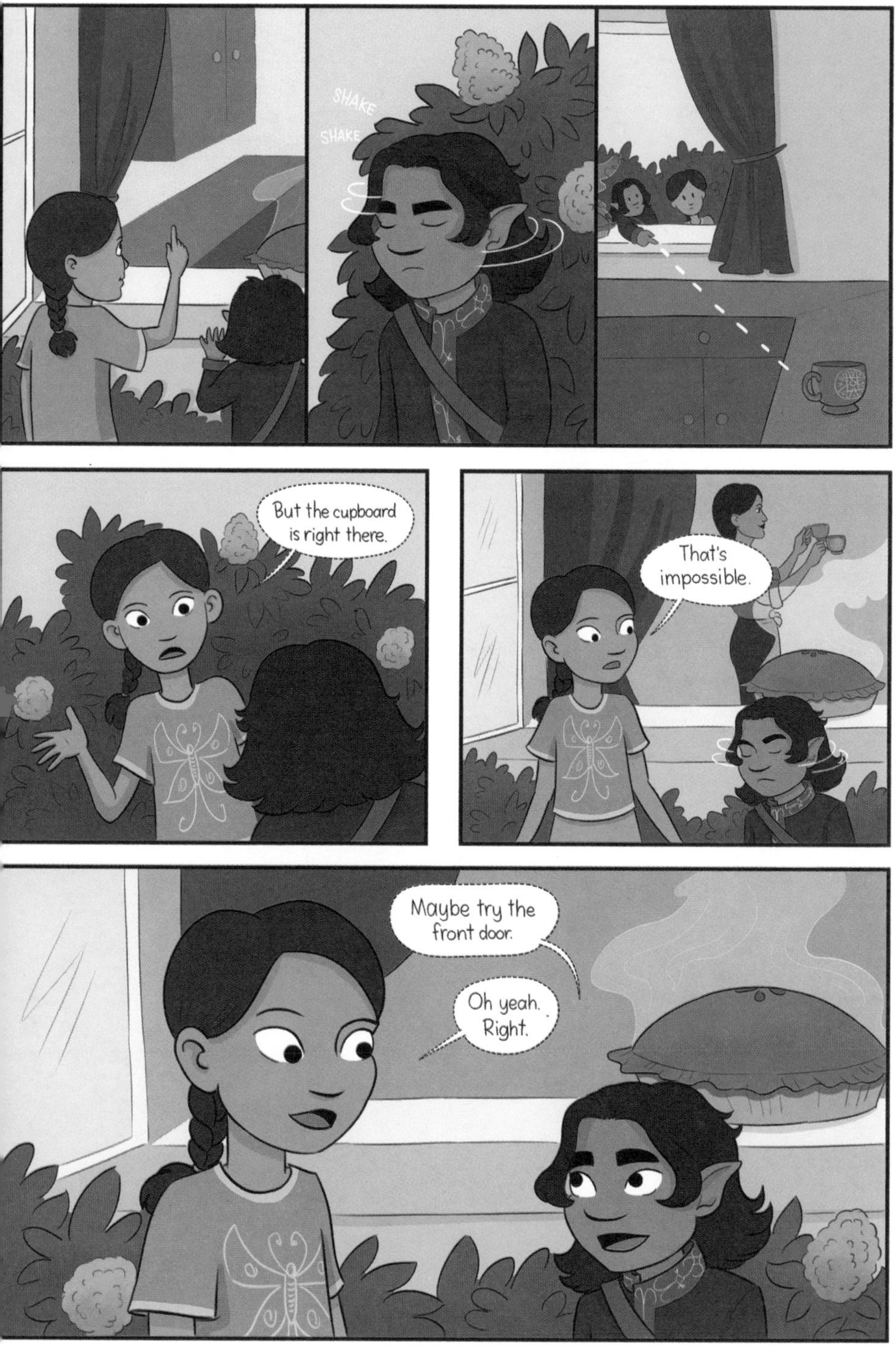
SHAKE
SHAKE
But the cupboard is right there.
That's impossible.
Maybe try the front door.
Oh yeah. Right.

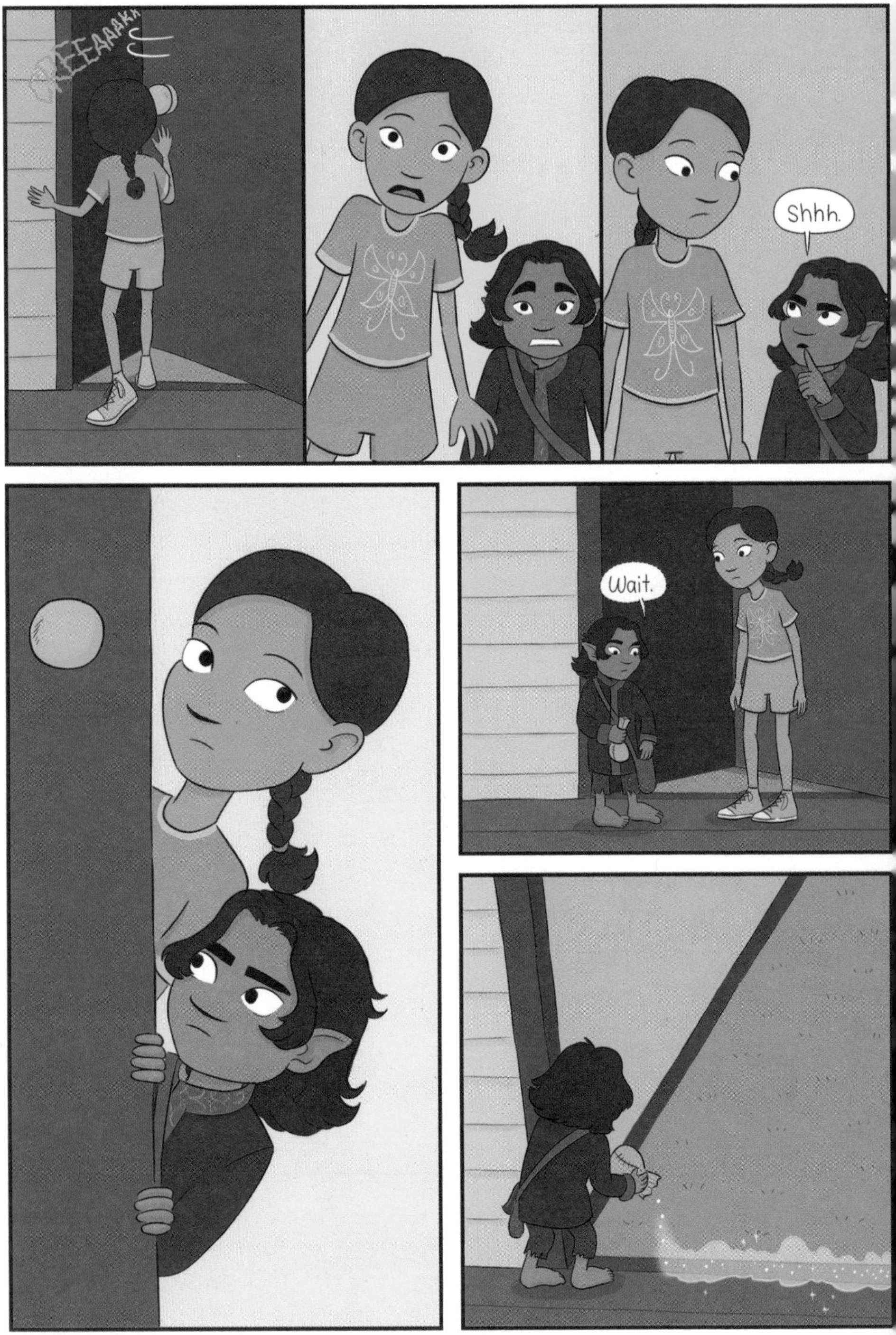
CREEAAAKK
Shhh.
Wait.

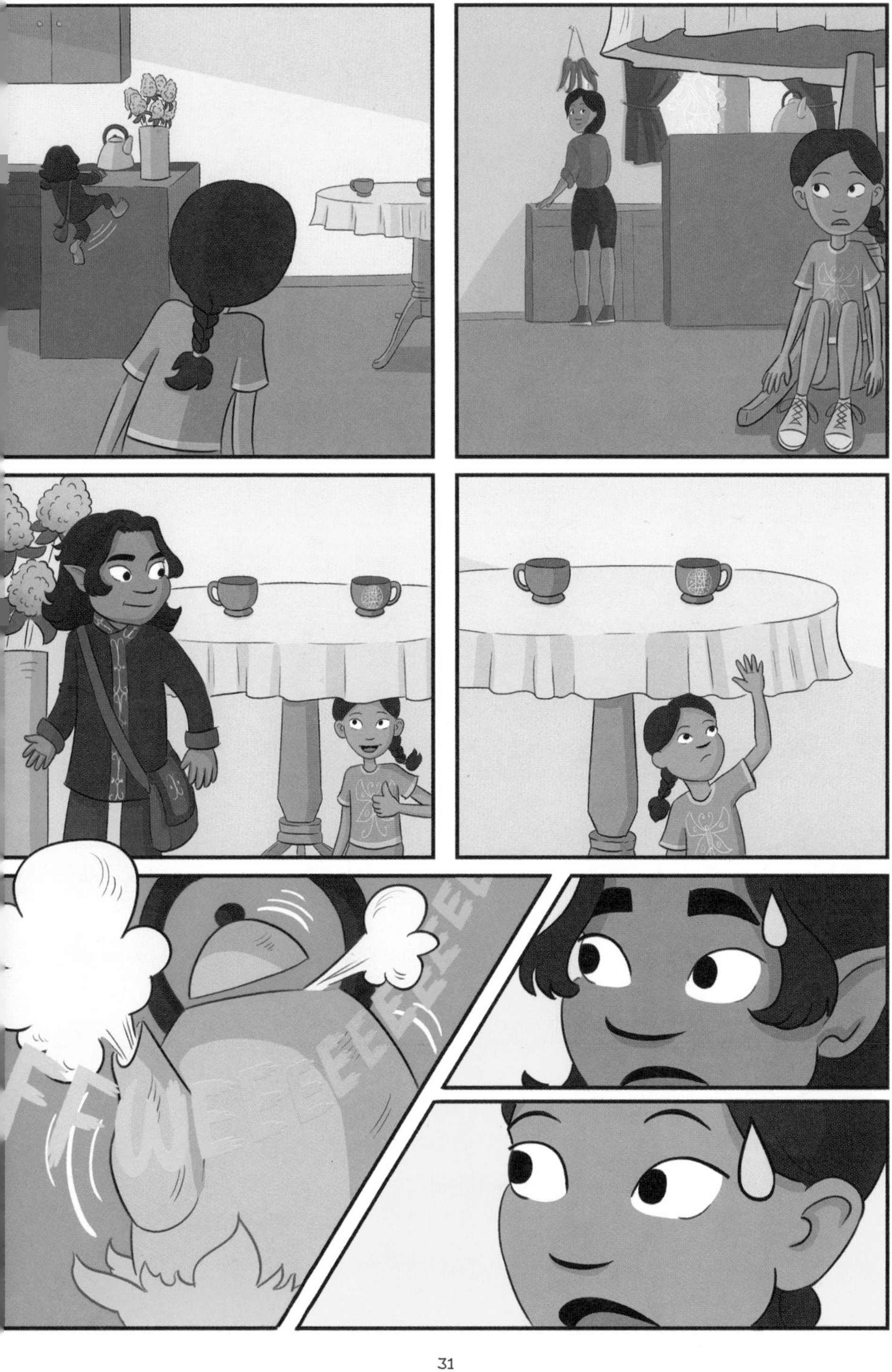
FFWEEEEEEEEE

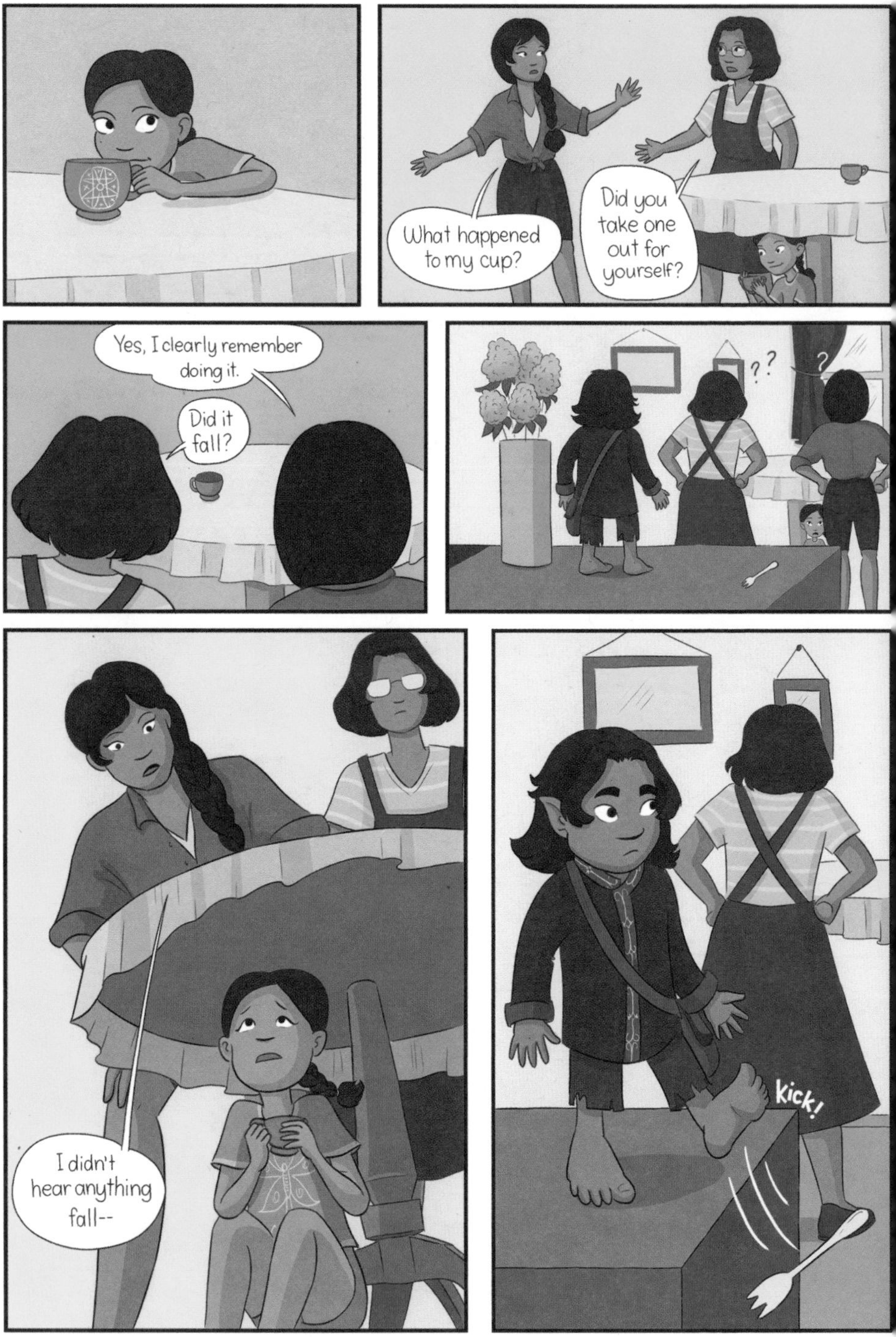
What happened to my cup?
Did you take one out for yourself?
Yes, I clearly remember doing it.
Did it fall?
??
?
I didn't hear anything fall--
KICK!

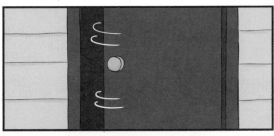

We did it! That was a close one!

Not bad, kid. You did pretty well back there.

With my help.

Now for the next item.

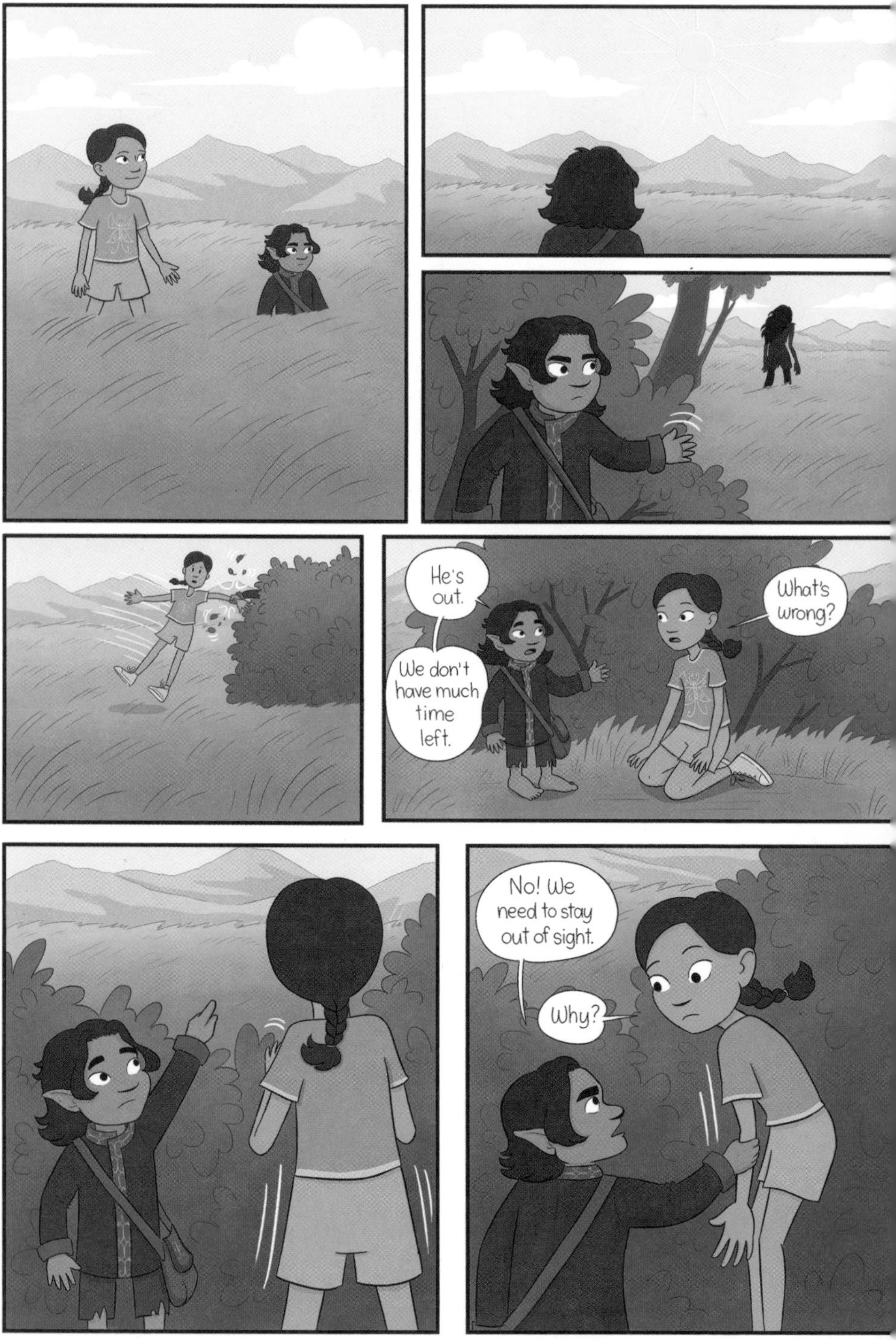
He's out.
We don't have much time left.
What's wrong?
No! We need to stay out of sight.
Why?

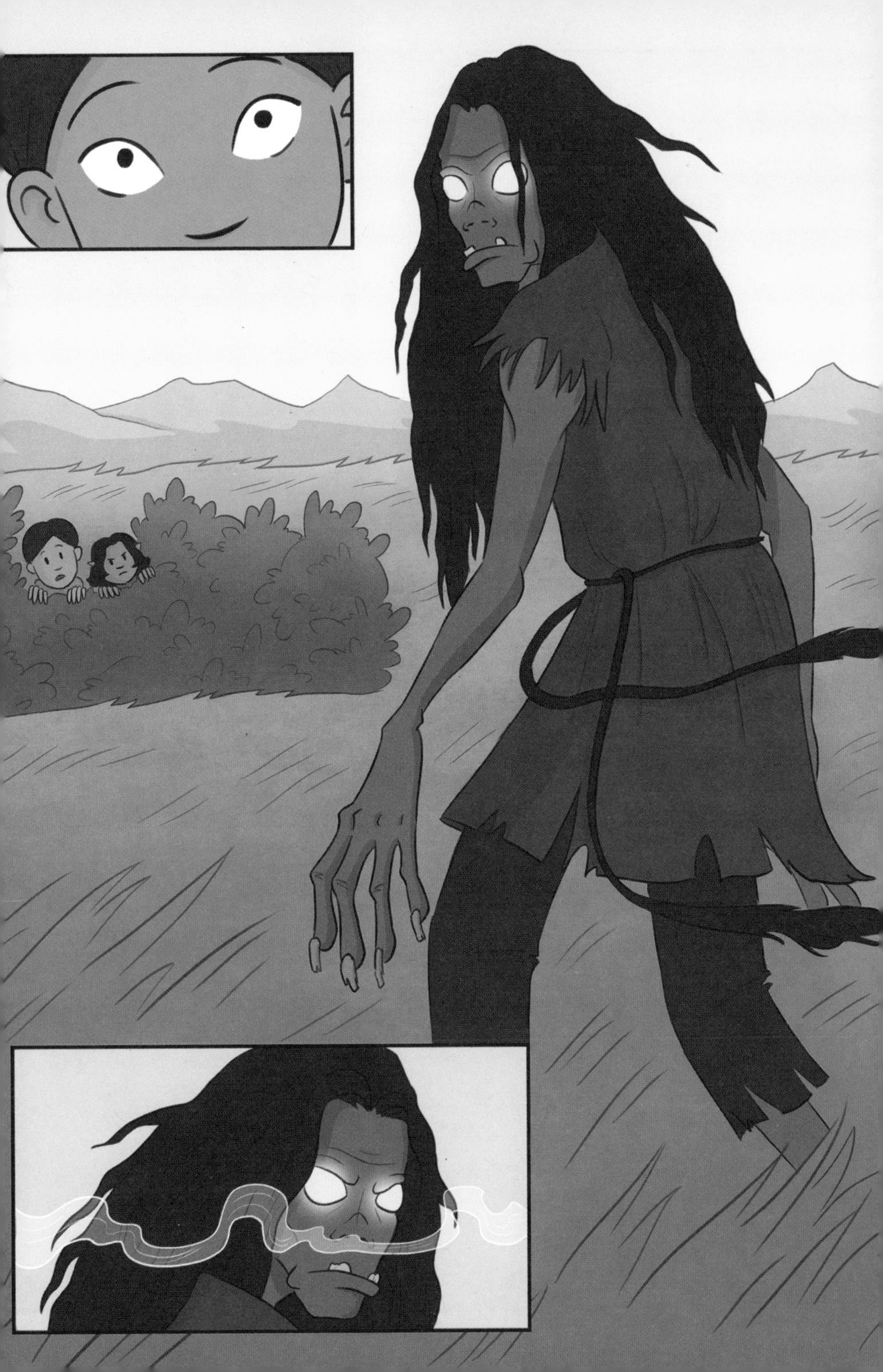

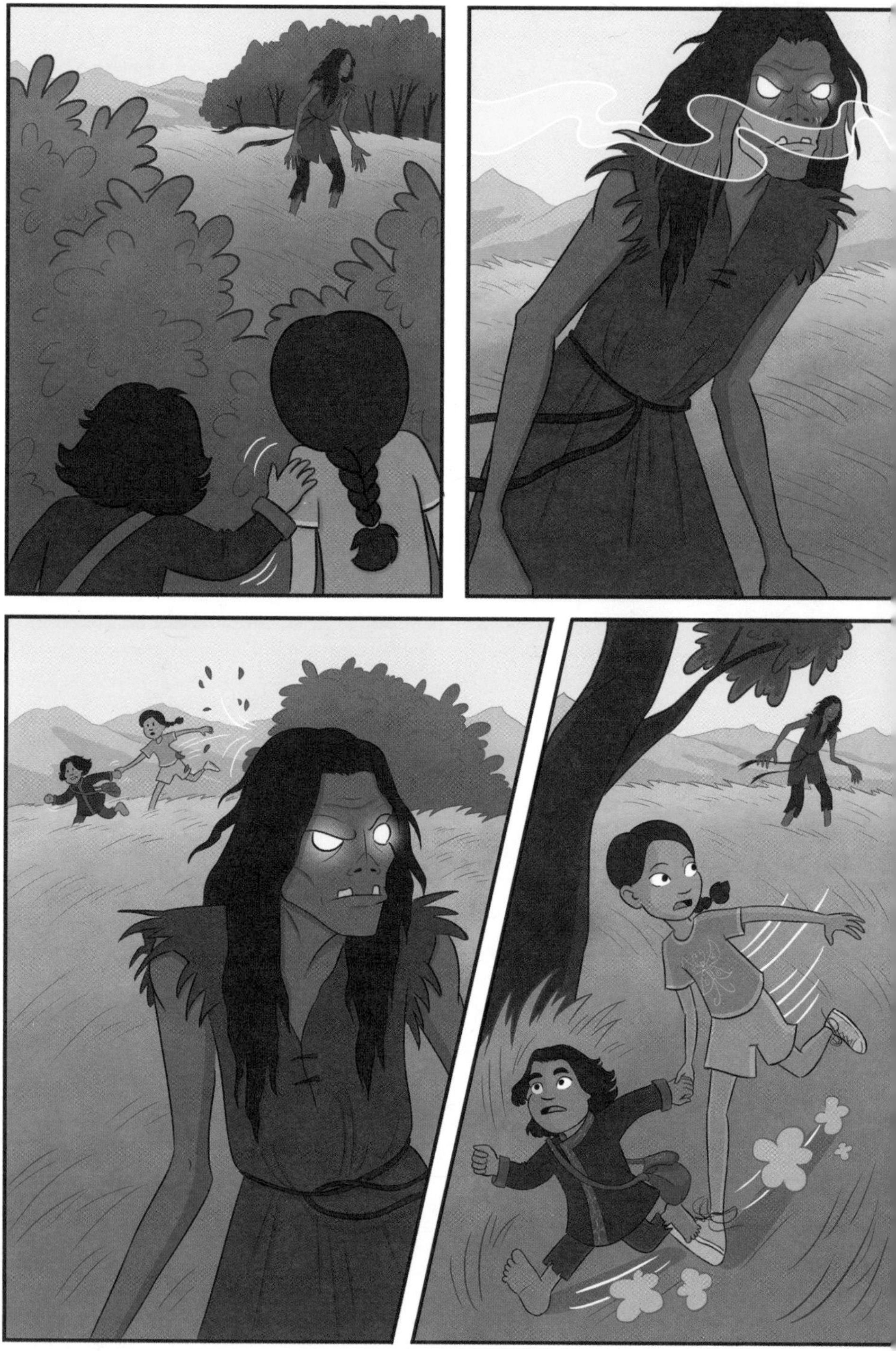

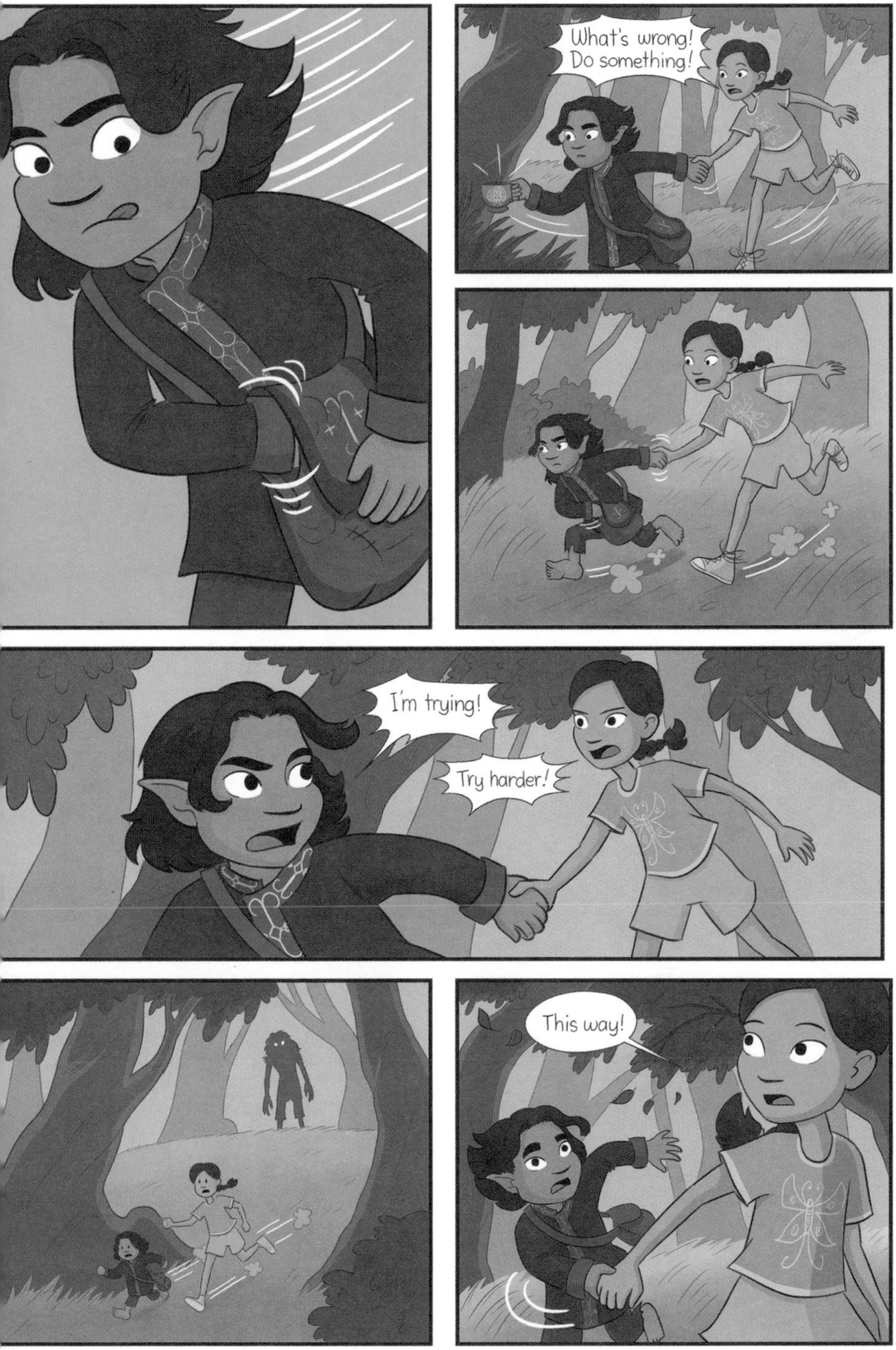

What's wrong!
Do something!
I'm trying!
Try harder!
This way!

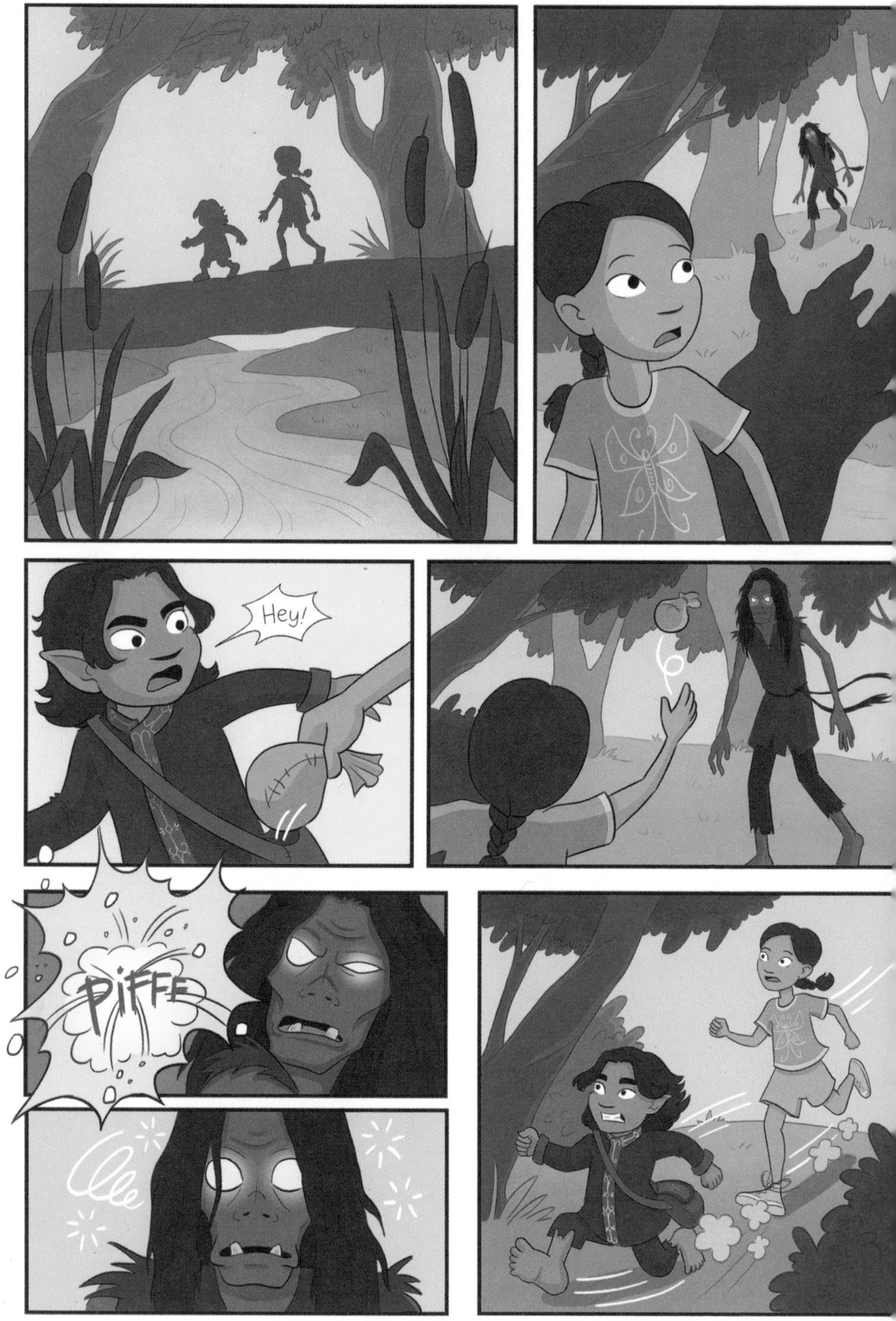
Hey!
PIFFF

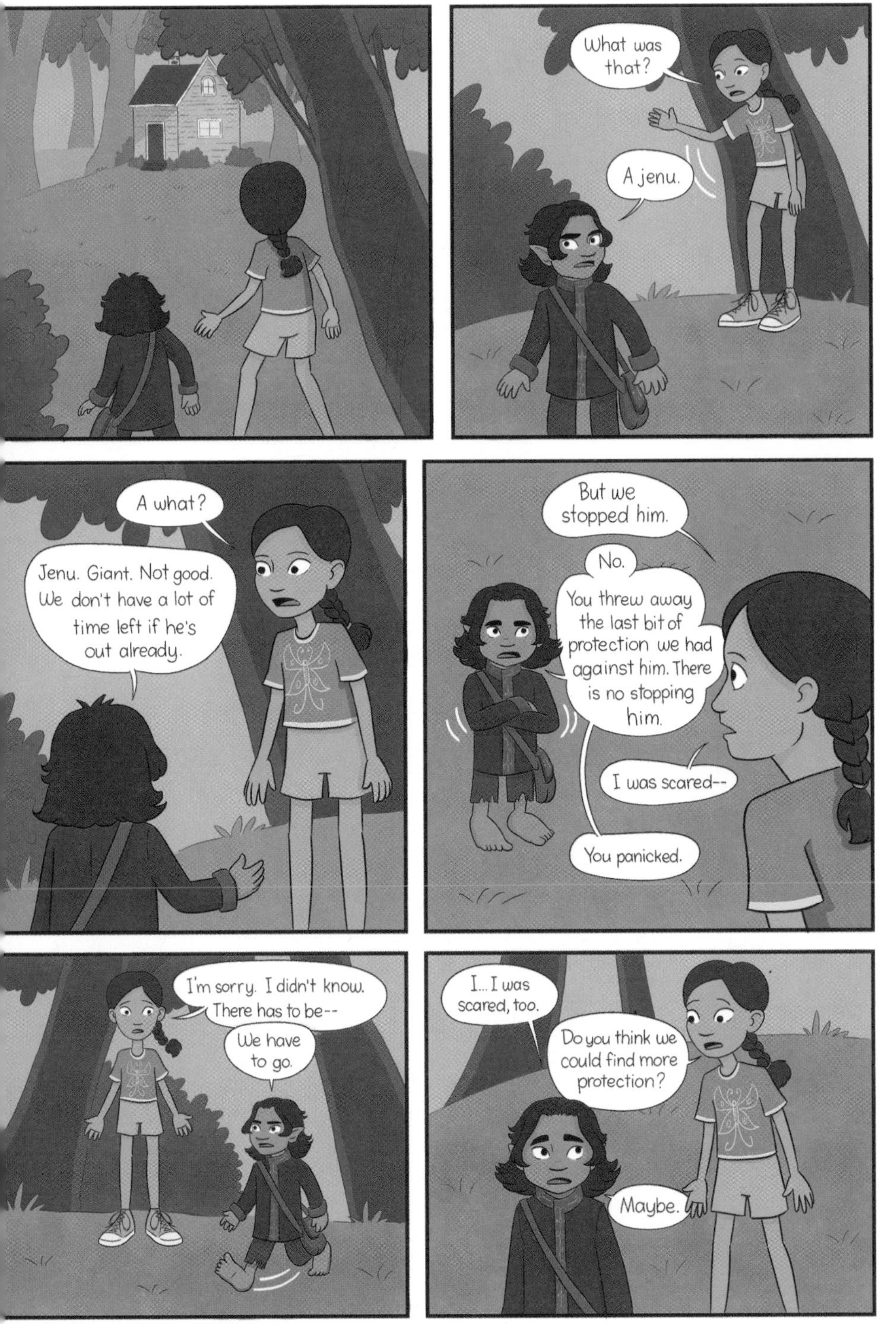
What was that?
A jenu.
A what?
Jenu. Giant. Not good. We don't have a lot of time left if he's out already.
But we stopped him.
No.
You threw away the last bit of protection we had against him. There is no stopping him.
I was scared--
You panicked.
I'm sorry. I didn't know. There has to be--
We have to go.
I... I was scared, too.
Do you think we could find more protection?
Maybe.

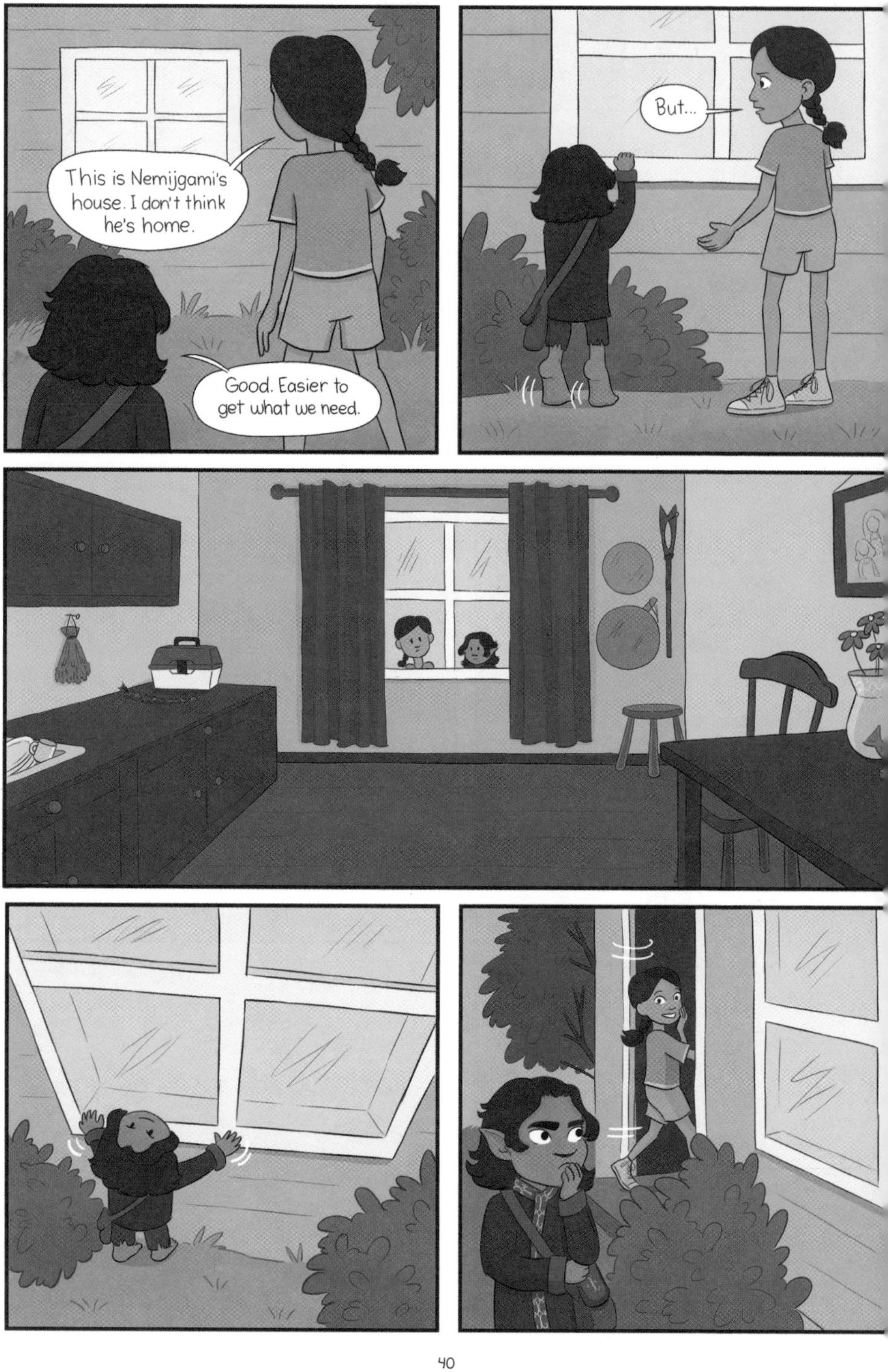
This is Nemijgami's house. I don't think he's home.
Good. Easier to get what we need.
But...

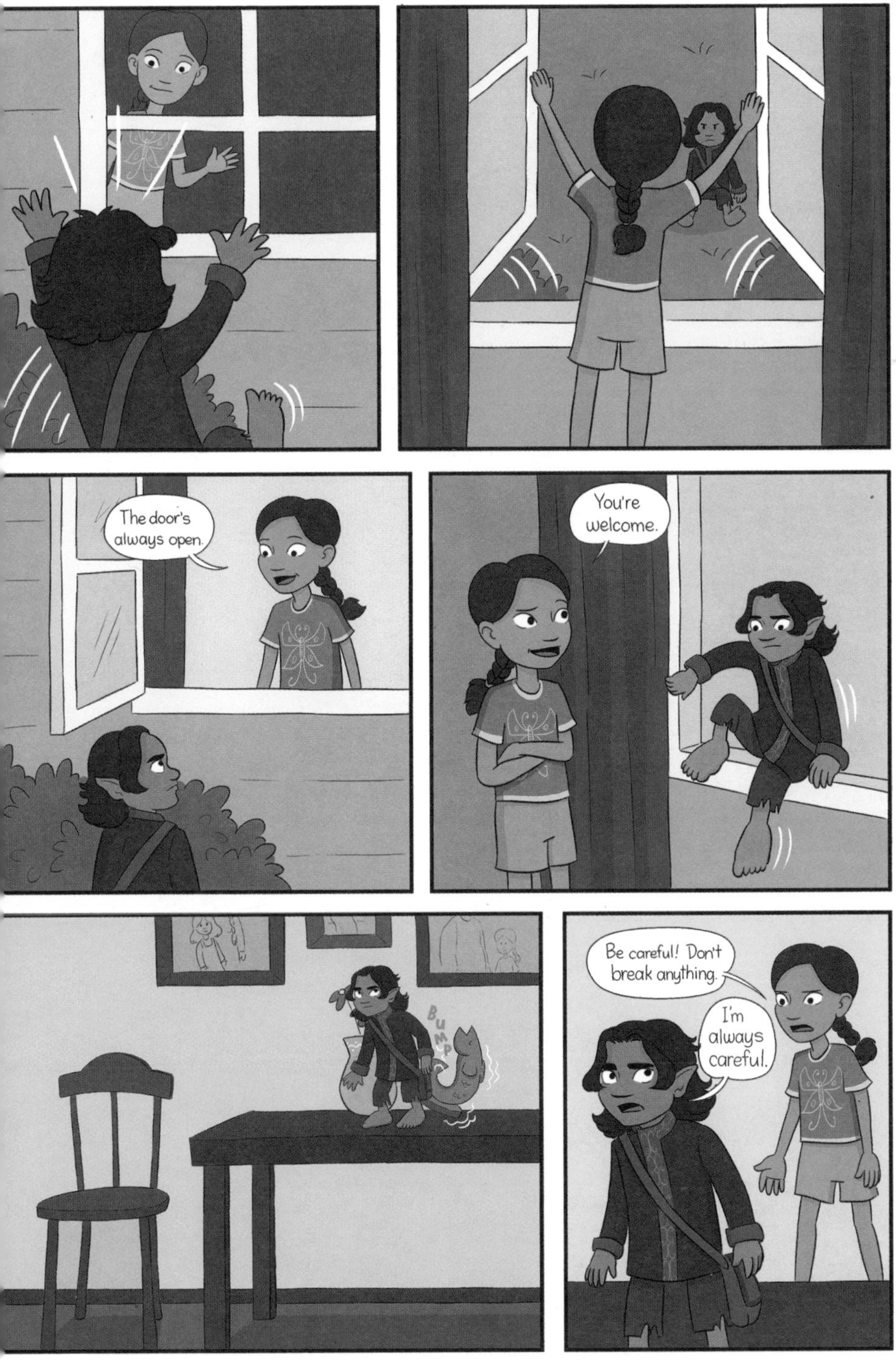
The door's always open.
You're welcome.
BUMP
Be careful! Don't break anything.
I'm always careful.

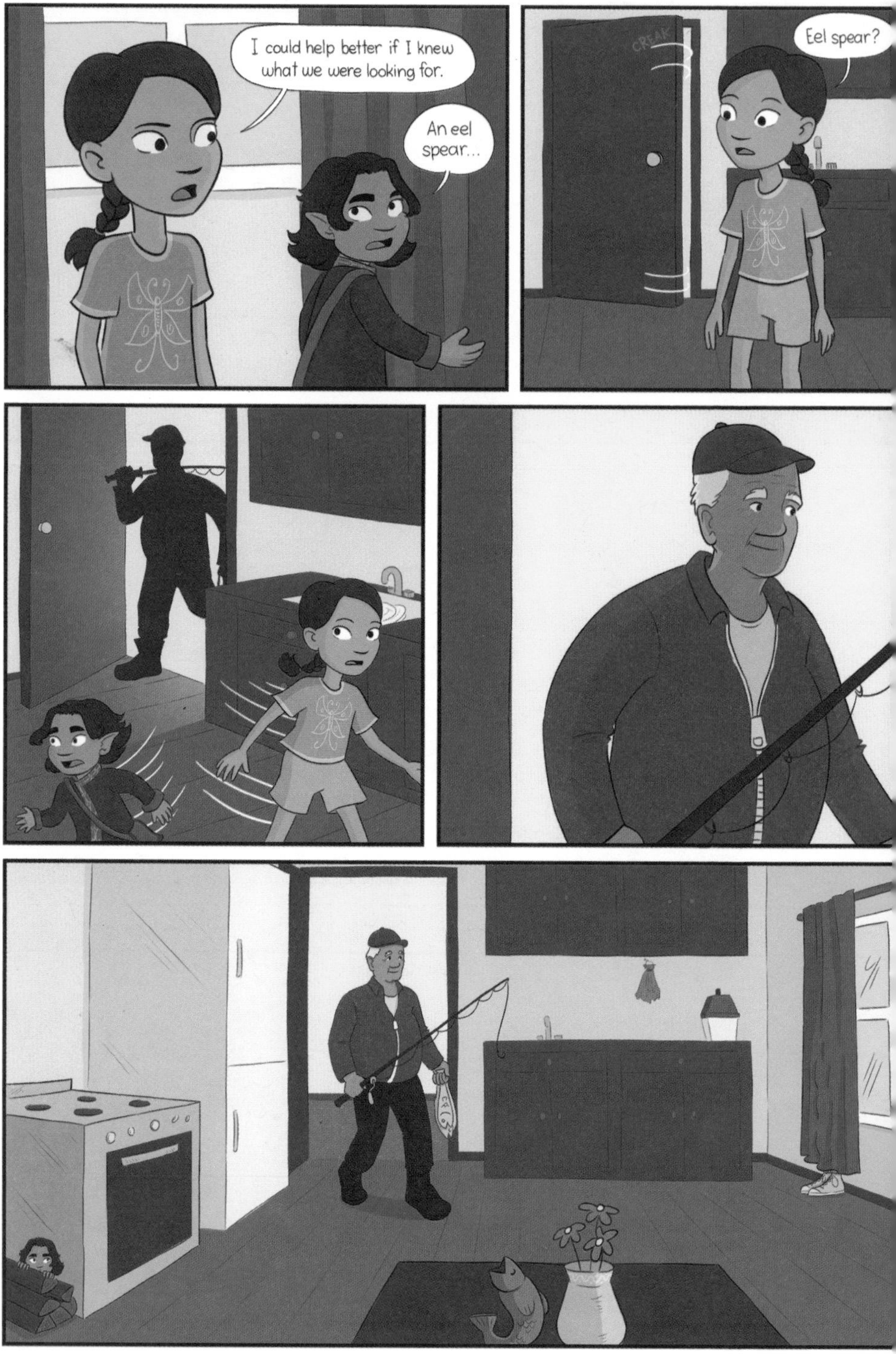
I could help better if I knew what we were looking for.
An eel spear...
CREAK
Eel spear?

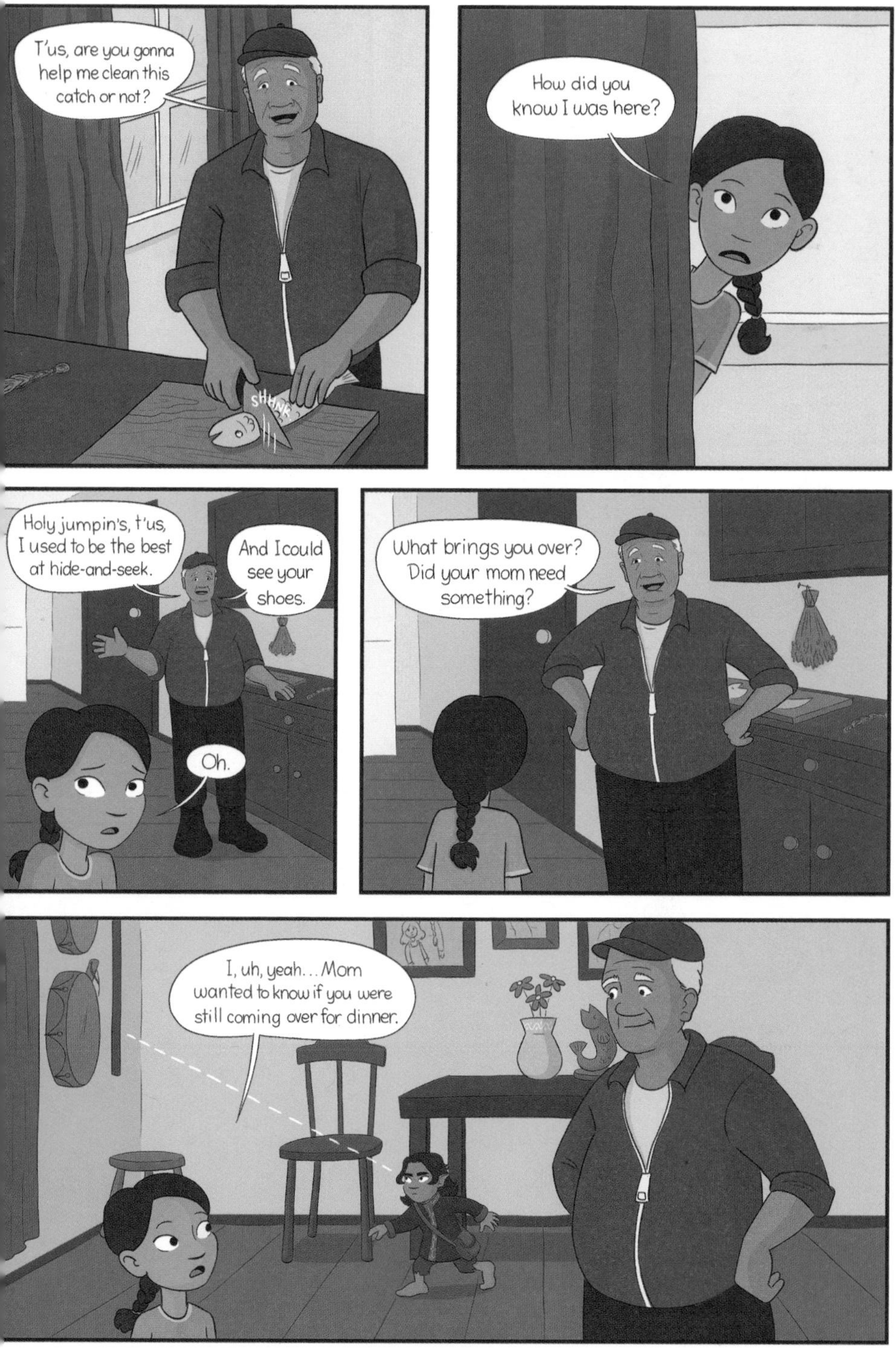
T'us, are you gonna help me clean this catch or not?
SHHNK
How did you know I was here?
Holy jumpin's, t'us, I used to be the best at hide-and-seek.
And I could see your shoes.
Oh.
What brings you over? Did your mom need something?
I, uh, yeah... Mom wanted to know if you were still coming over for dinner.

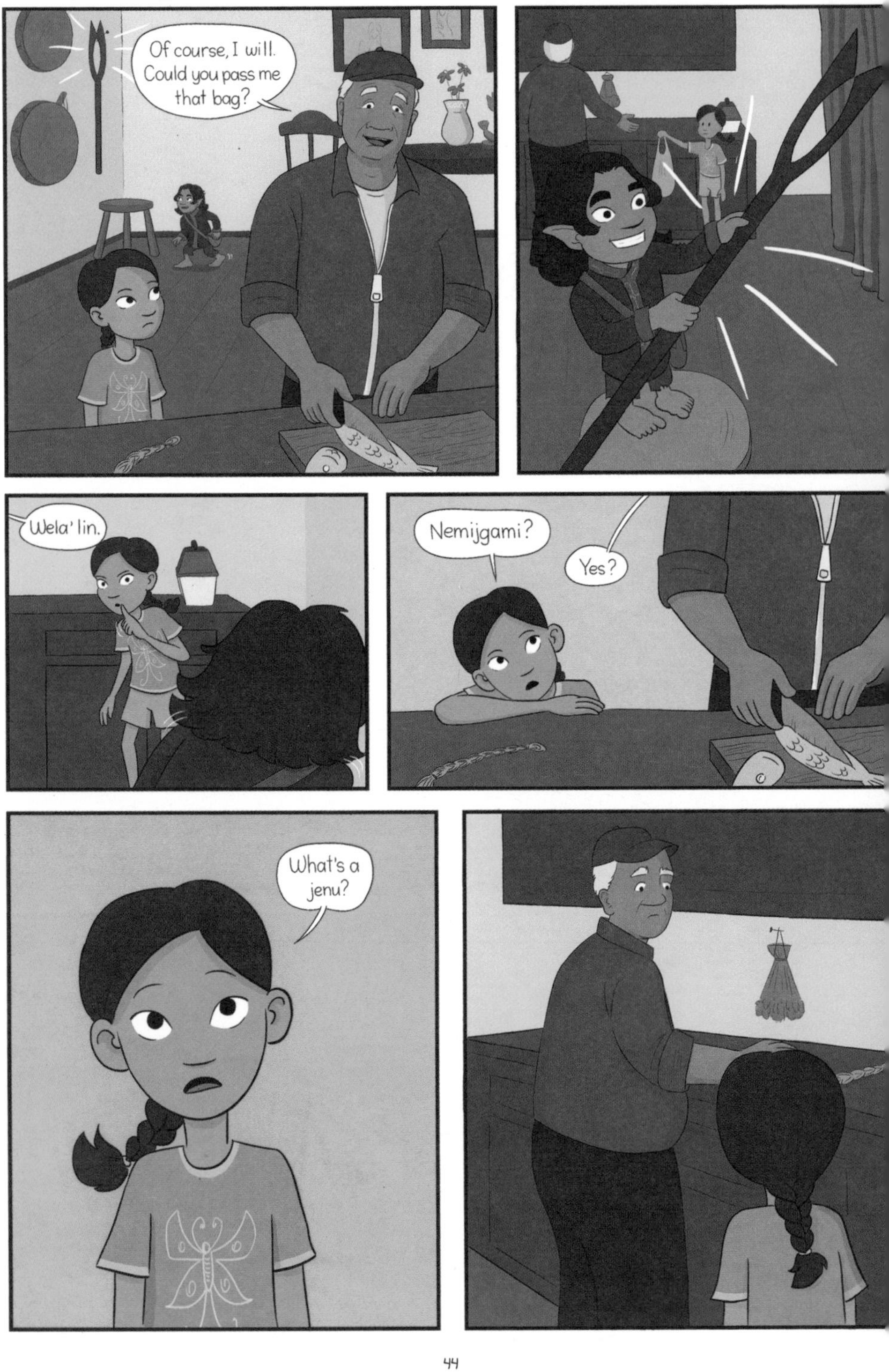

Of course, I will. Could you pass me that bag?
Wela'lin.
Nemijgami?
Yes?
What's a jenu?

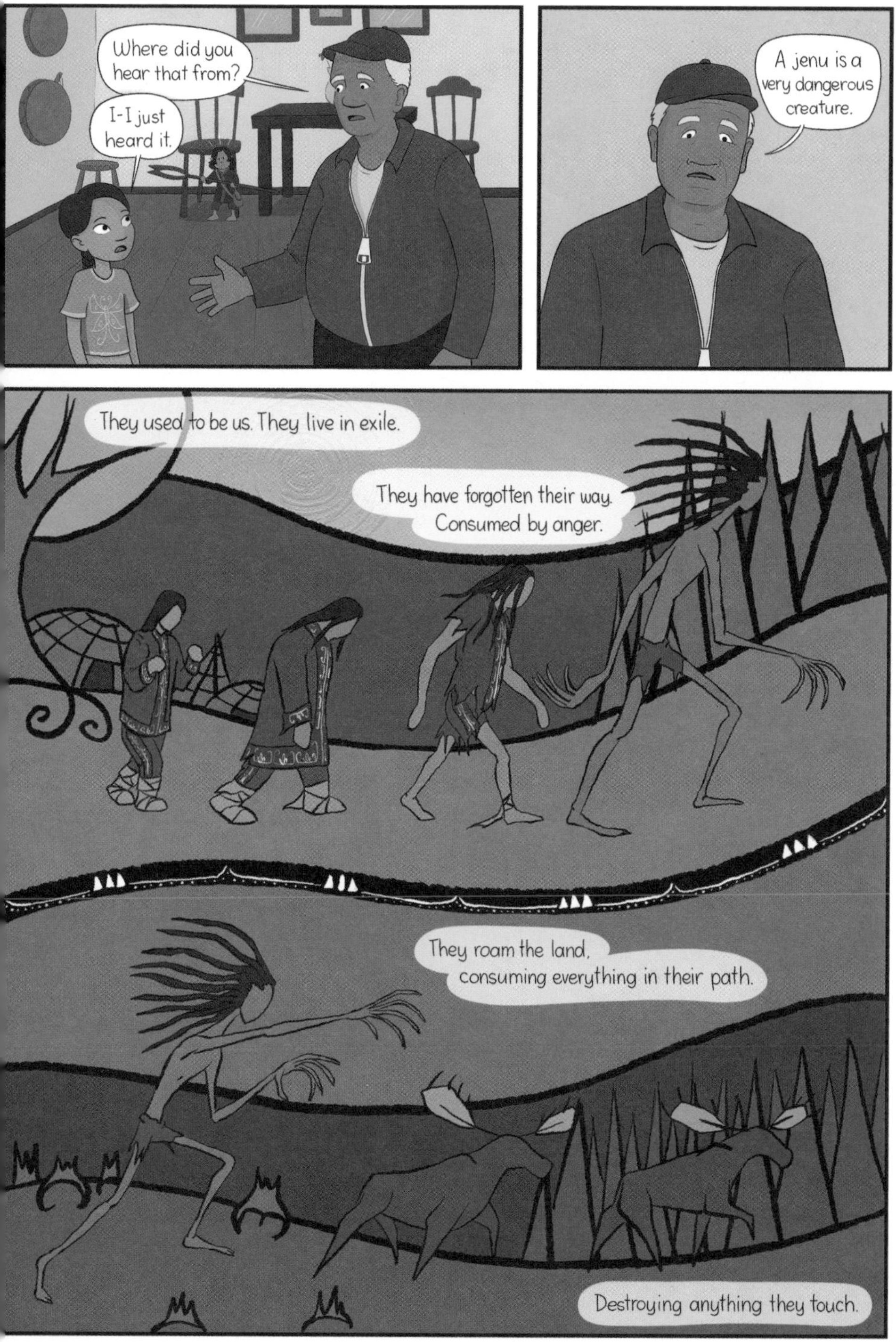
Where did you hear that from?
I-I just heard it.
A jenu is a very dangerous creature.
They used to be us. They live in exile.
They have forgotten their way. Consumed by anger.
They roam the land, consuming everything in their path.
Destroying anything they touch.

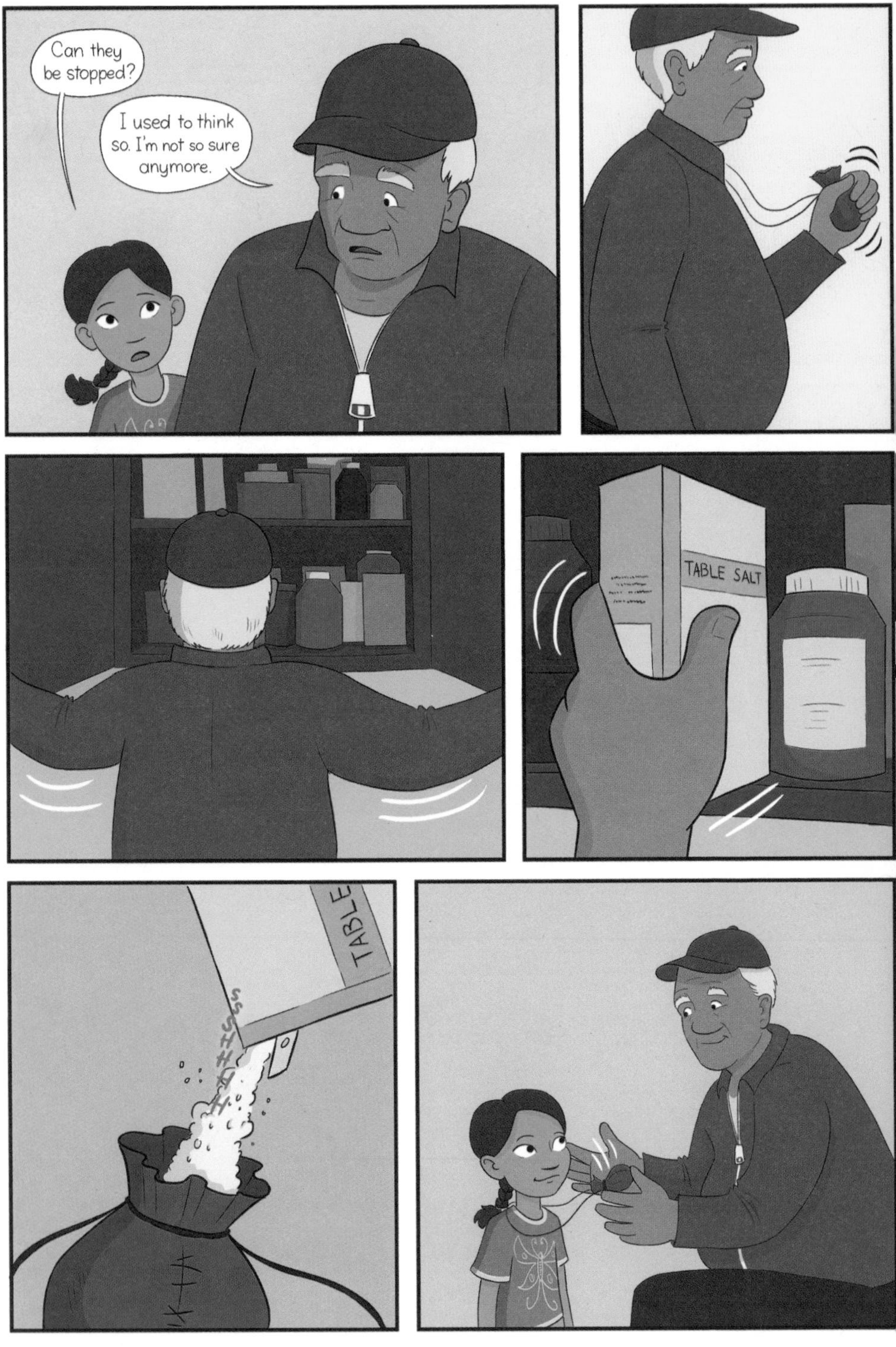
Can they be stopped?
I used to think so. I'm not so sure anymore.
TABLE SALT
TABLE

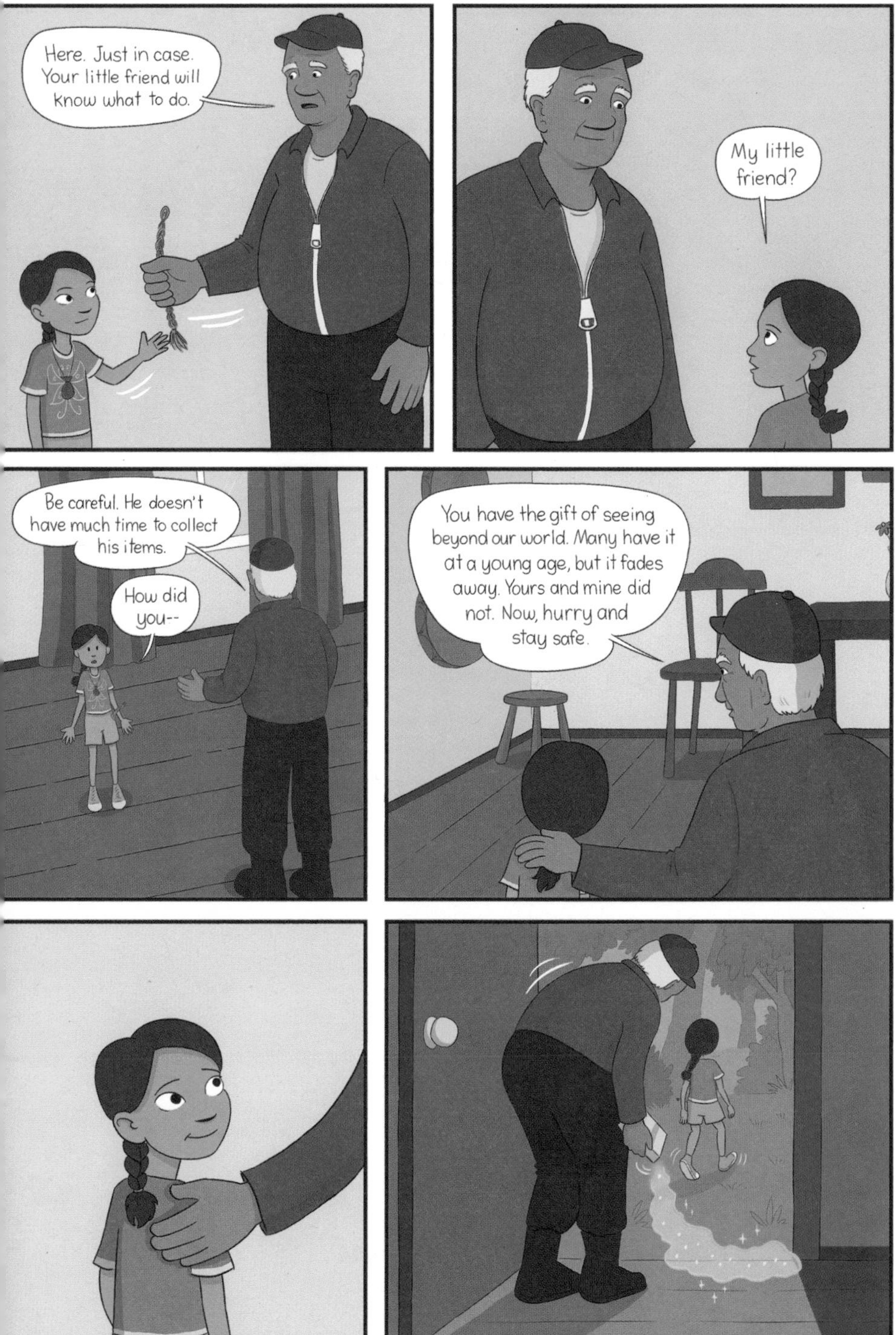
Here. Just in case. Your little friend will know what to do.
My little friend?
Be careful. He doesn't have much time to collect his items.
How did you--
You have the gift of seeing beyond our world. Many have it at a young age, but it fades away. Yours and mine did not. Now, hurry and stay safe.

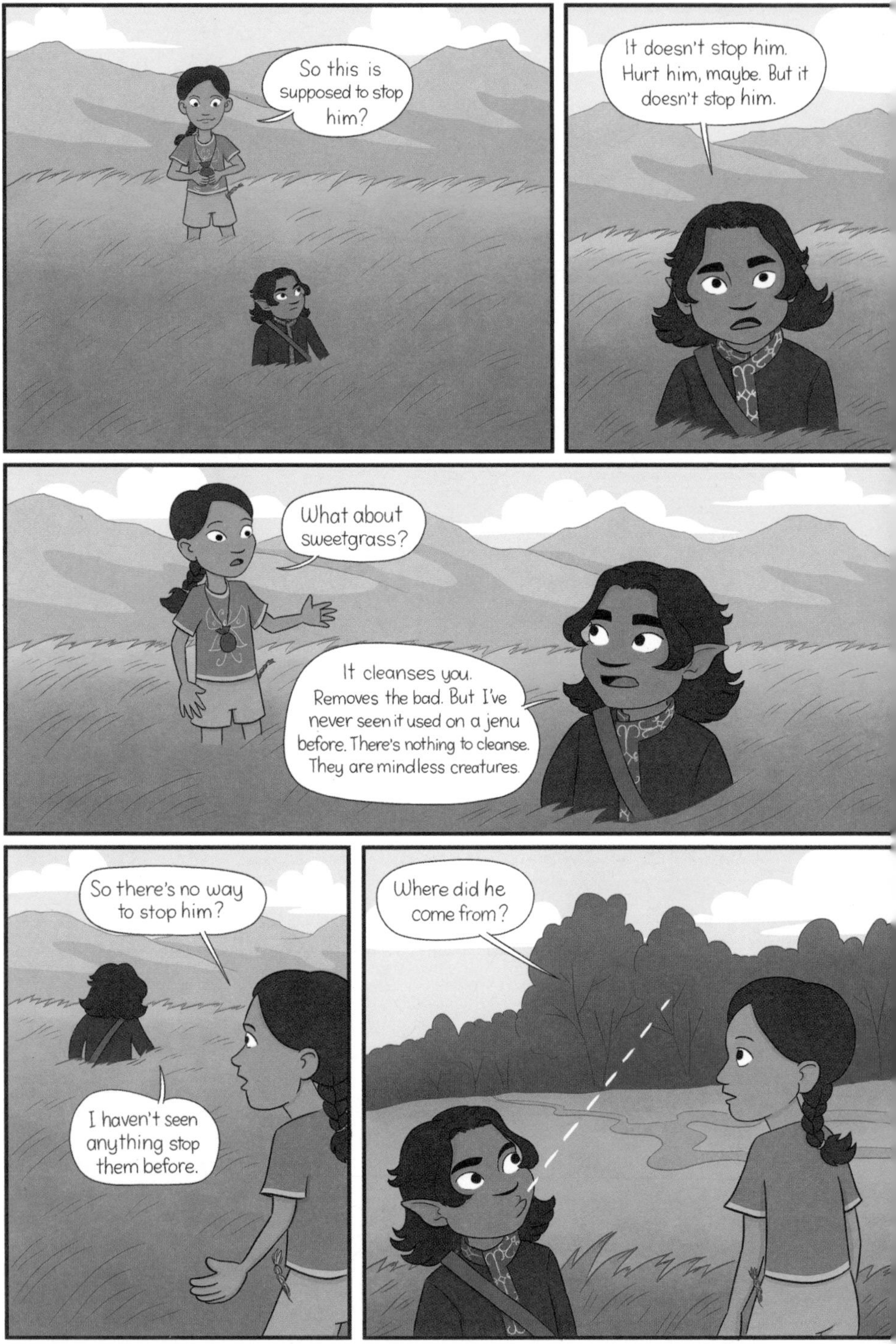
So this is supposed to stop him?
It doesn't stop him. Hurt him, maybe. But it doesn't stop him.
What about sweetgrass?
It cleanses you. Removes the bad. But I've never seen it used on a jenu before. There's nothing to cleanse. They are mindless creatures.
So there's no way to stop him?
I haven't seen anything stop them before.
Where did he come from?

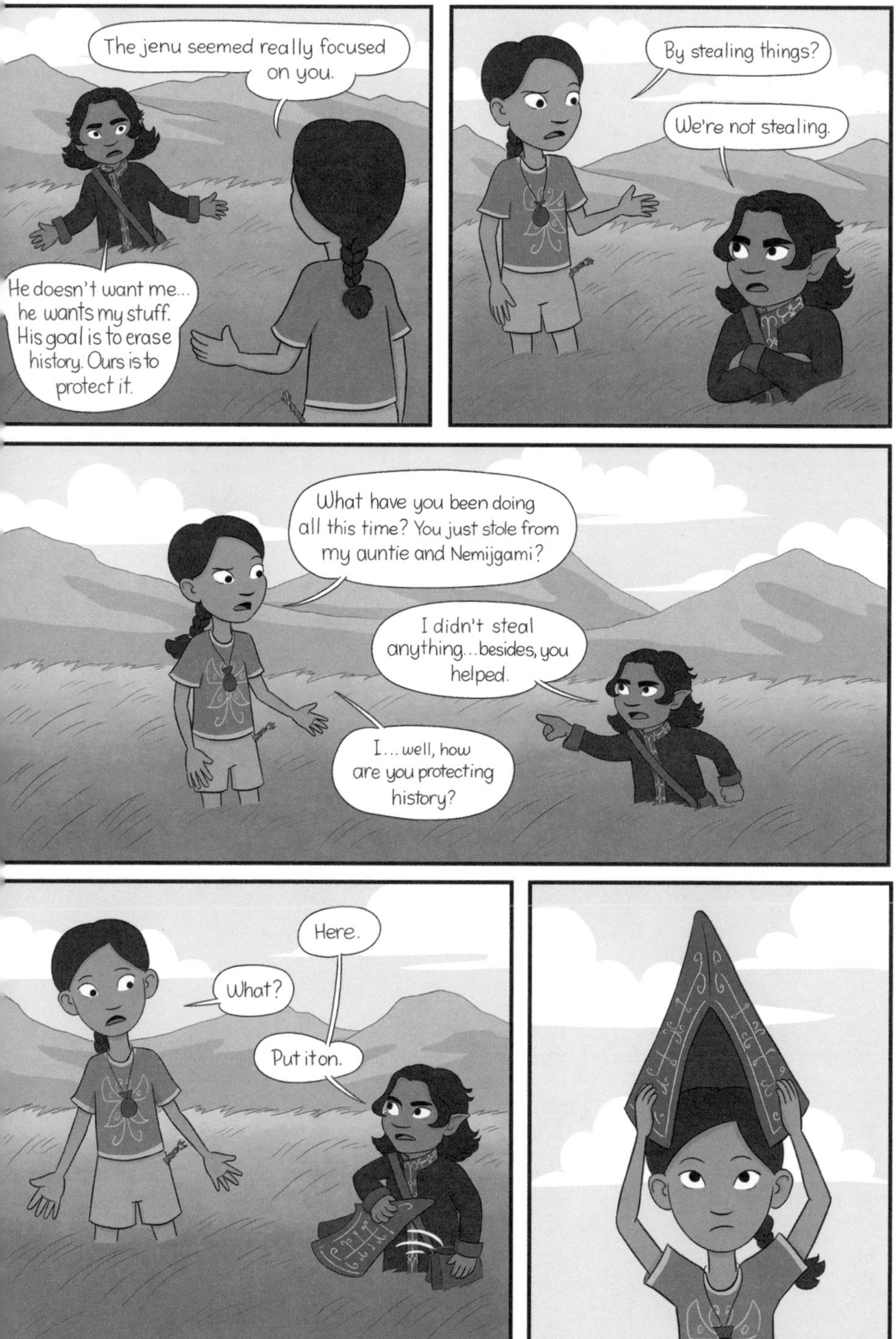

The jenu seemed really focused on you.
He doesn't want me... he wants my stuff. His goal is to erase history. Ours is to protect it.
By stealing things?
We're not stealing.
What have you been doing all this time? You just stole from my auntie and Nemijgami?
I didn't steal anything...besides, you helped.
I... well, how are you protecting history?
Here.
What?
Put it on.

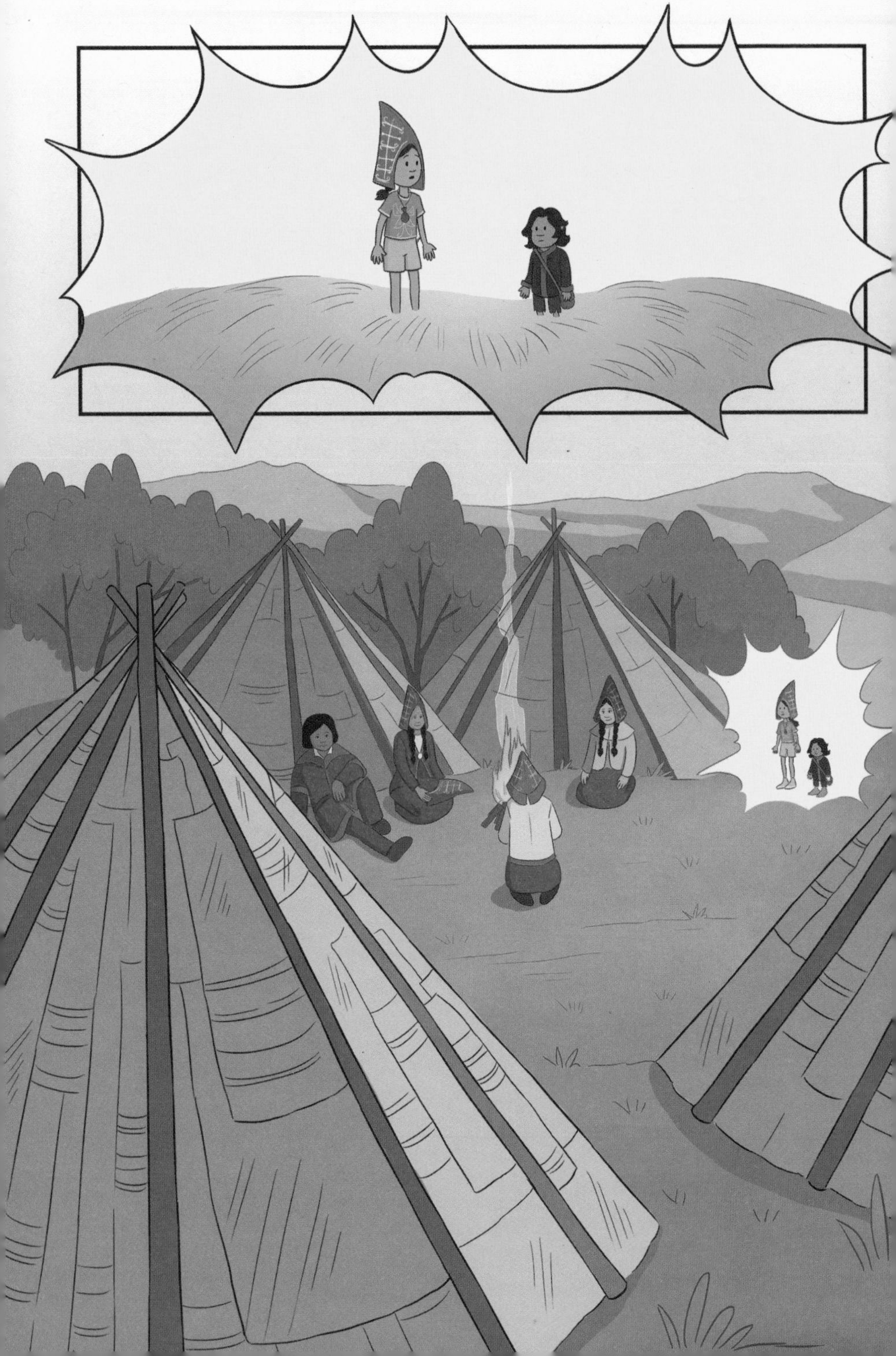

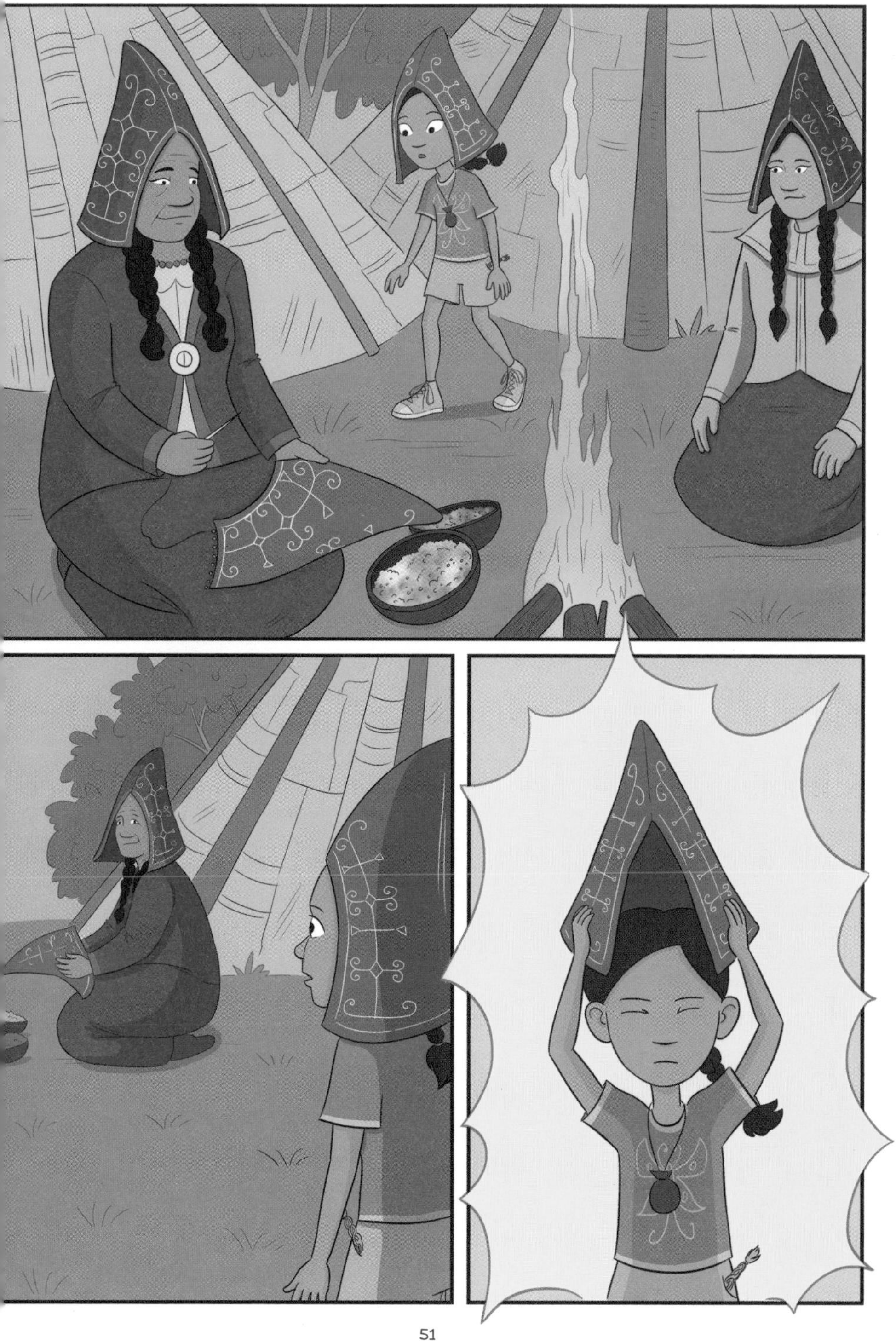

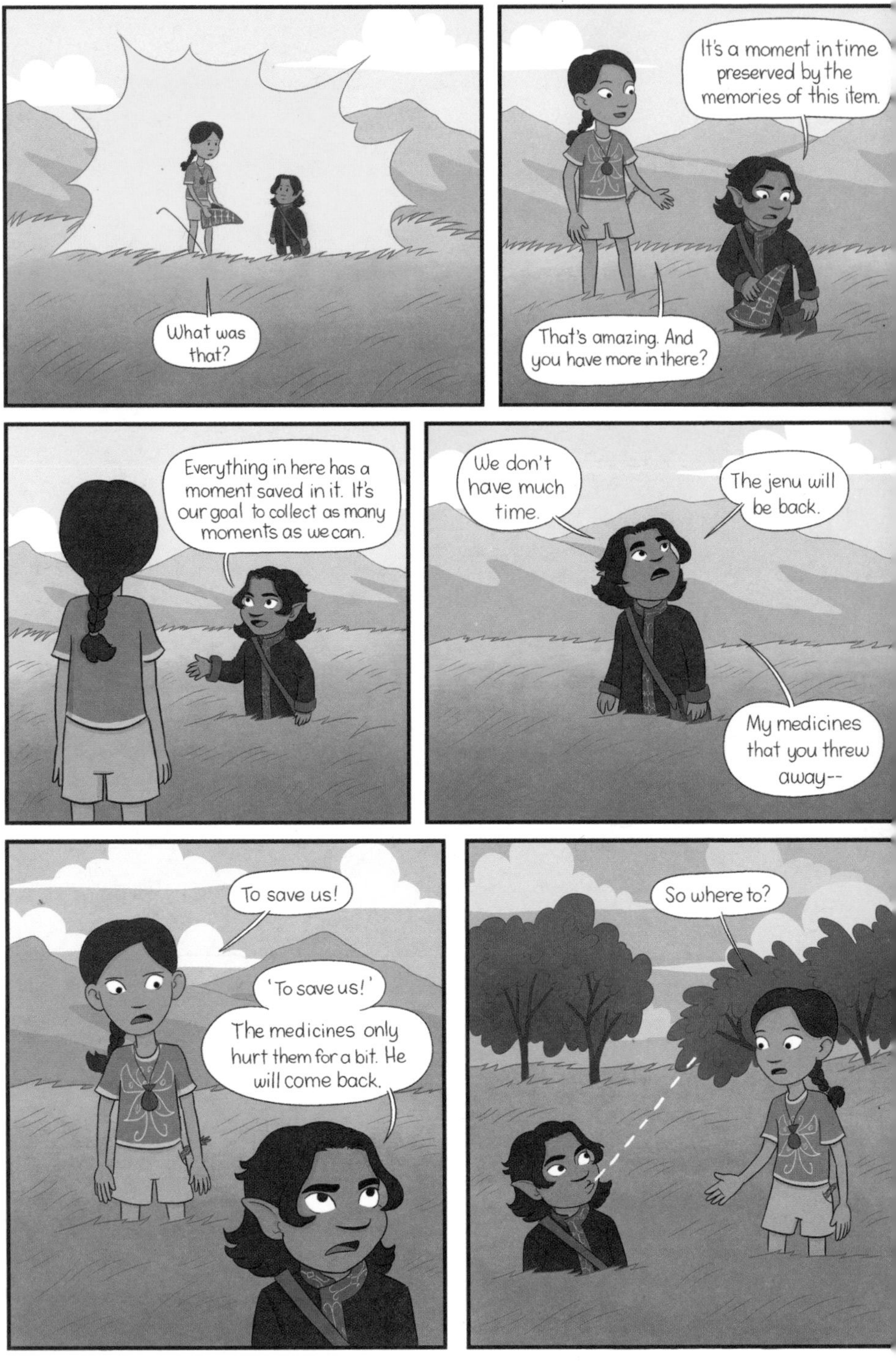
What was that?
It's a moment in time preserved by the memories of this item.
That's amazing. And you have more in there?
Everything in here has a moment saved in it. It's our goal to collect as many moments as we can.
We don't have much time.
The jenu will be back.
My medicines that you threw away--
To save us!
'To save us!'
The medicines only hurt them for a bit. He will come back.
So where to?

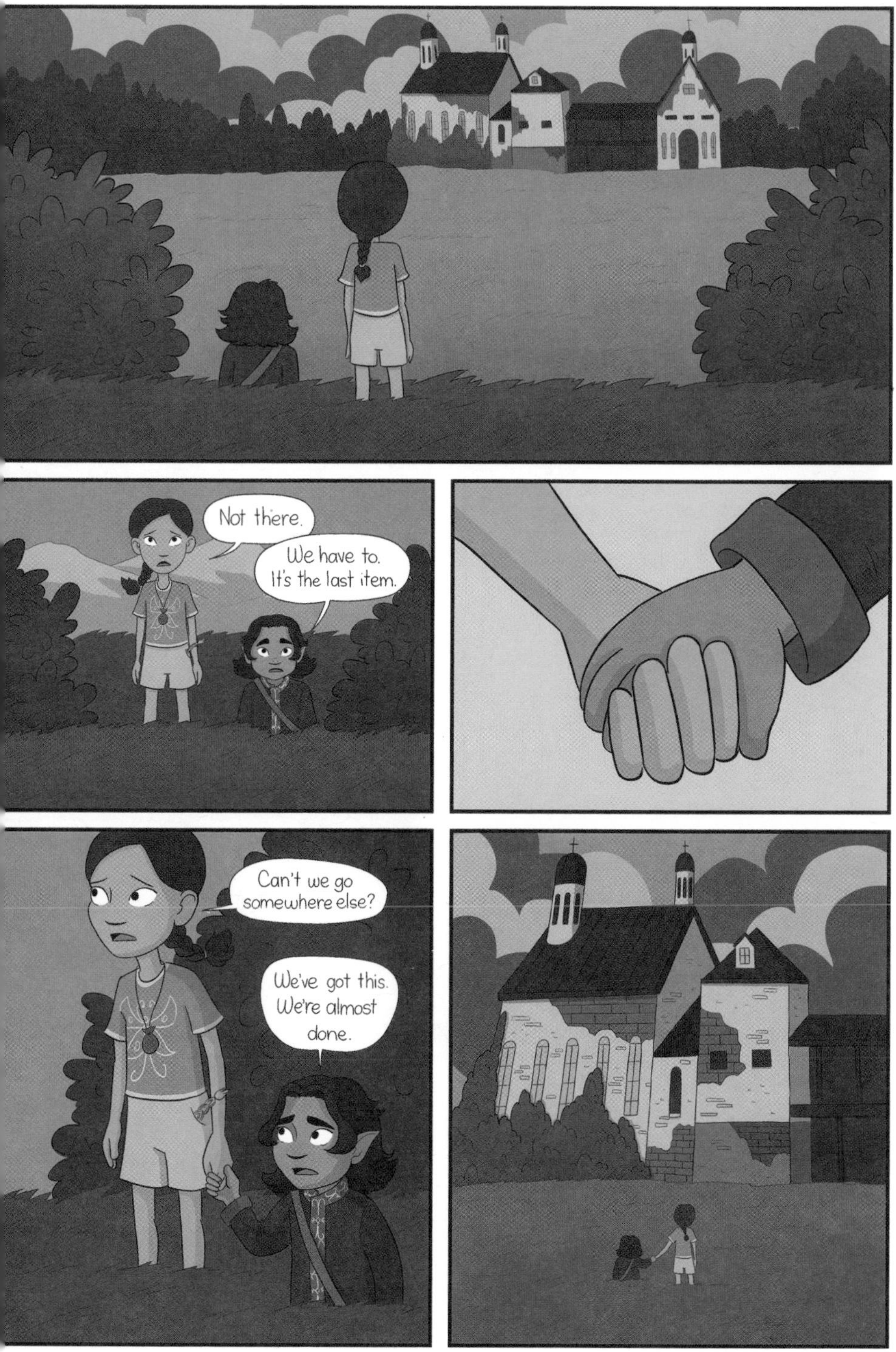
Not there.
We have to. It's the last item.
Can't we go somewhere else?
We've got this. We're almost done.

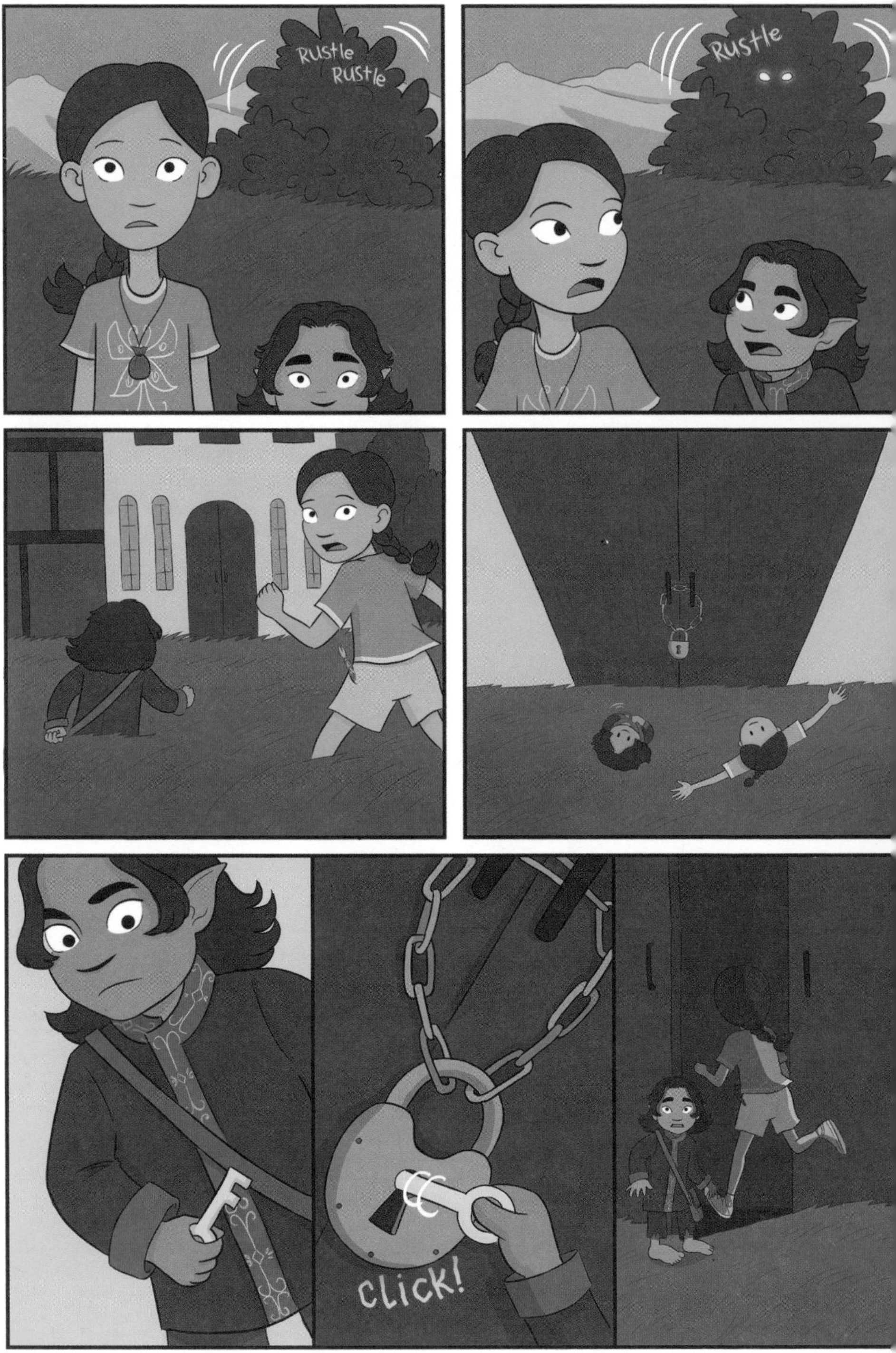
Rustle
Rustle
Rustle
CLICK!

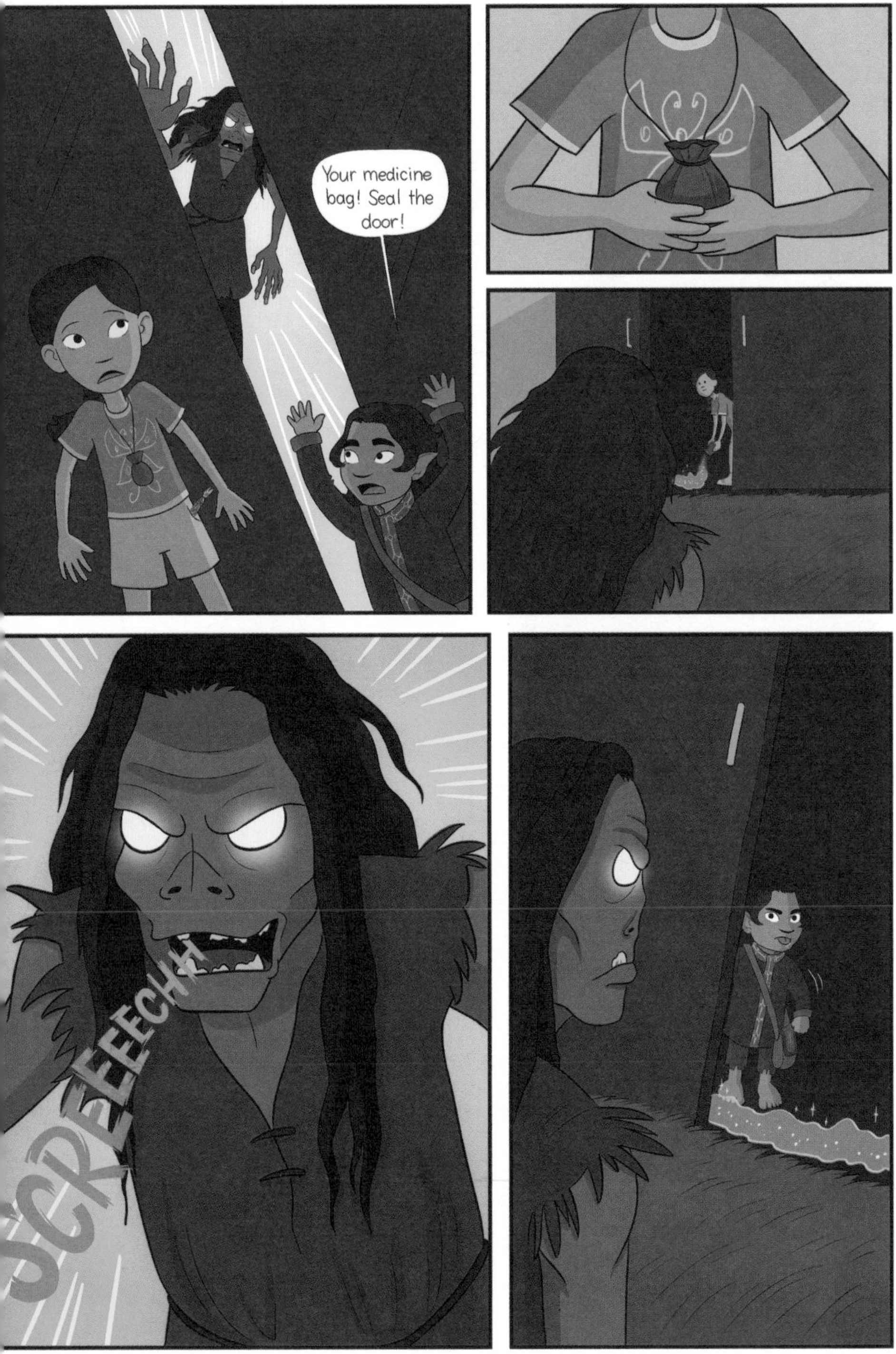
Your medicine bag! Seal the door!
SCREEEECHH

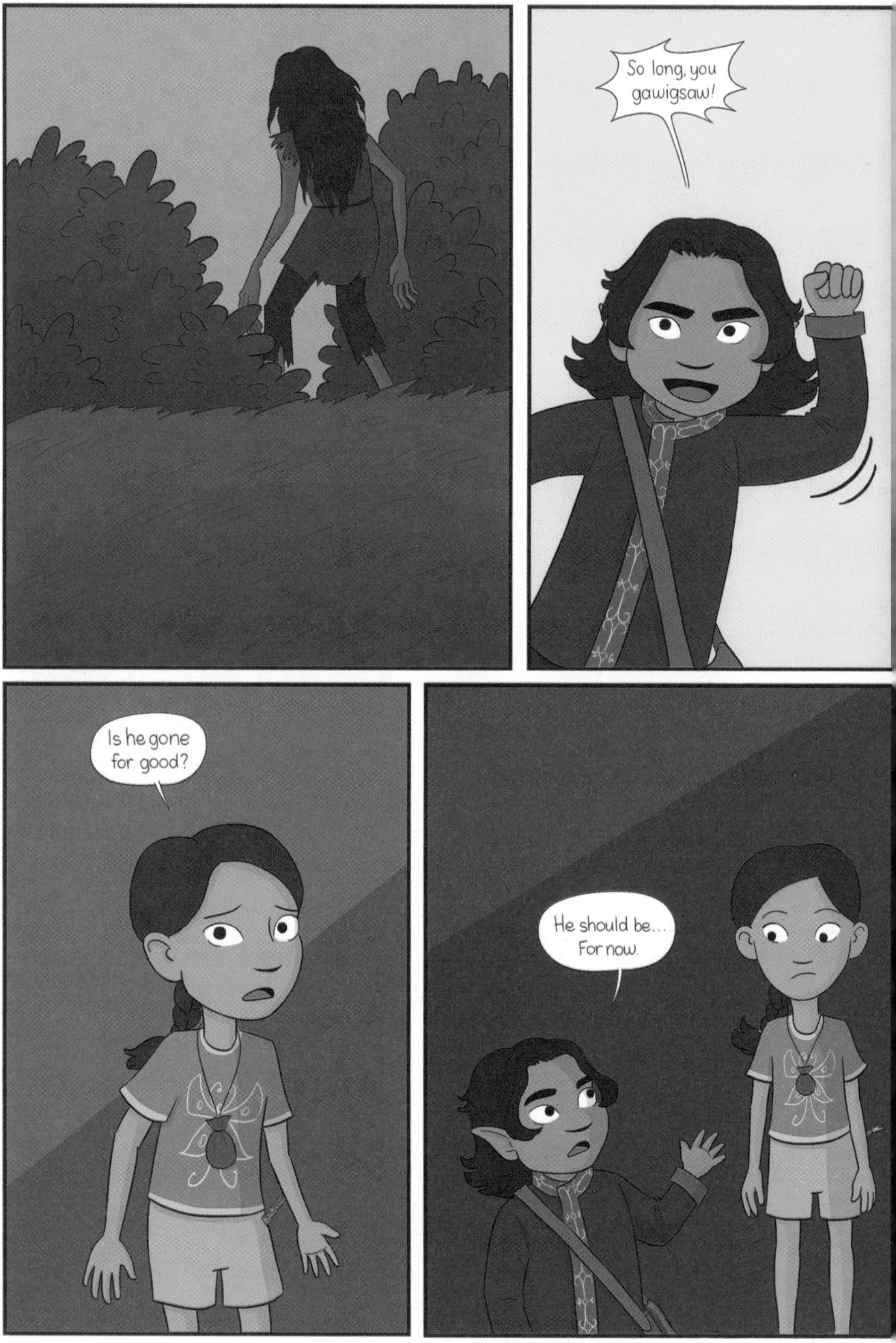
So long, you gawigsaw!
Is he gone for good?
He should be... For now.

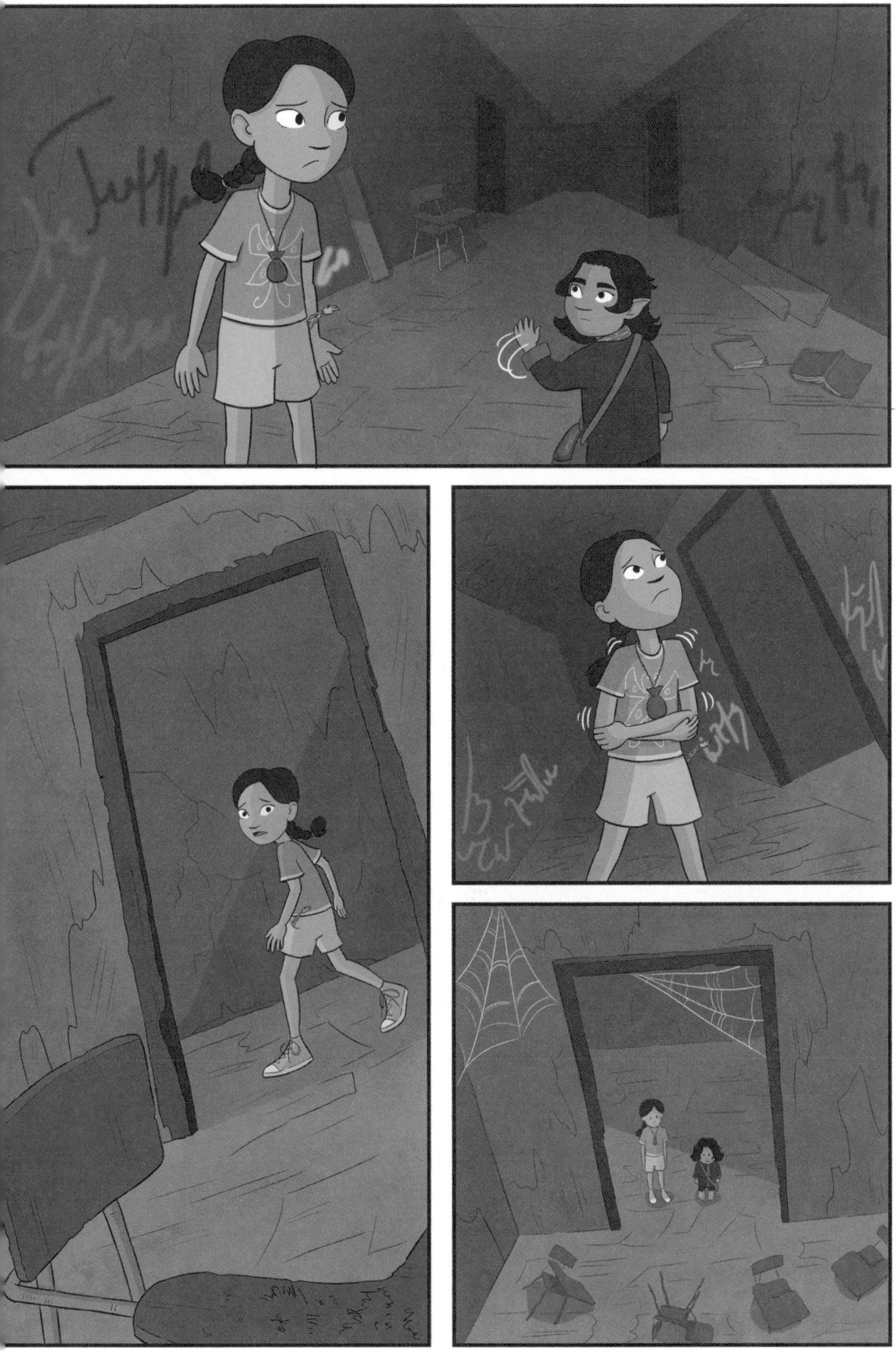

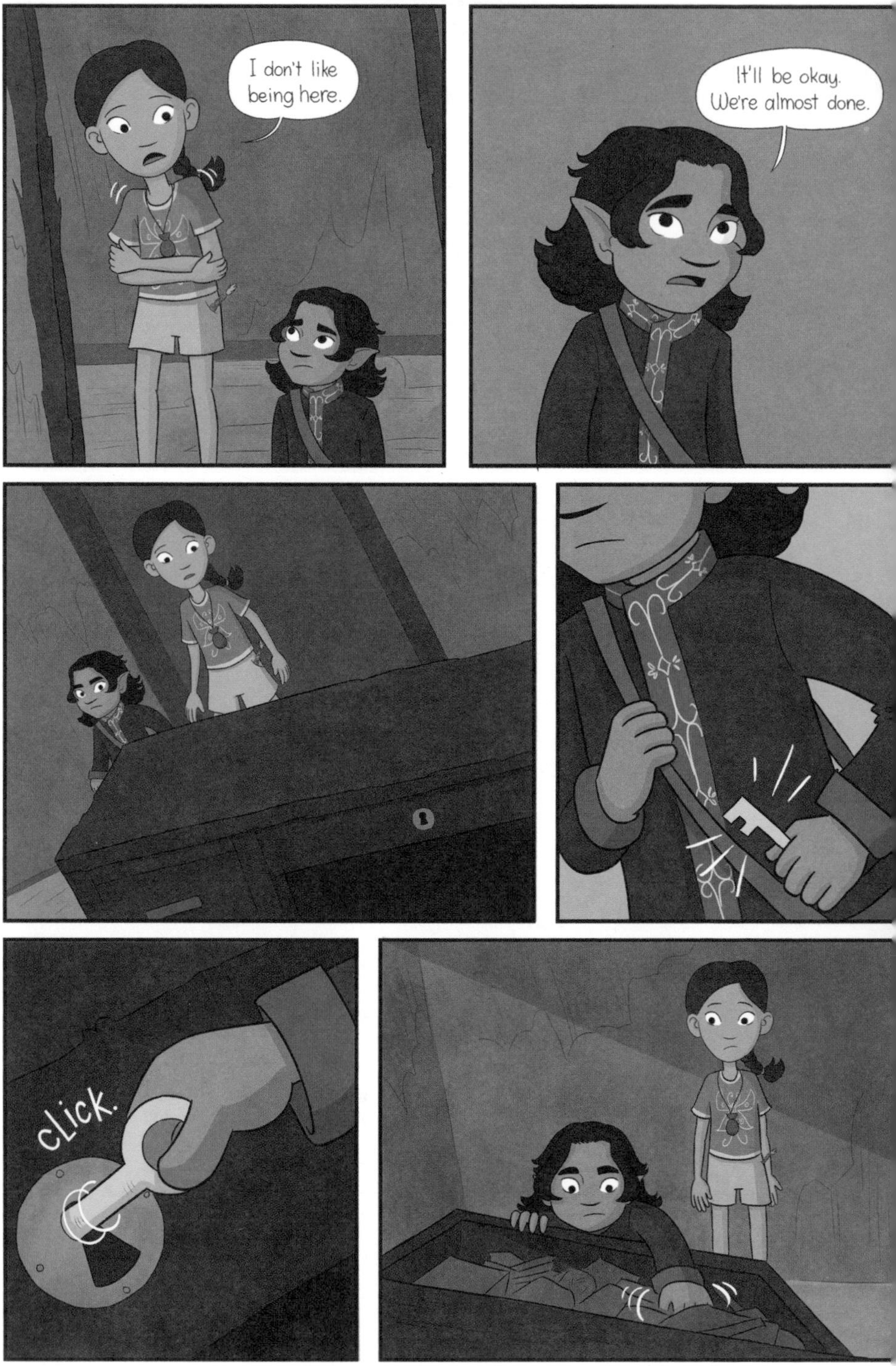
I don't like being here.
It'll be okay. We're almost done.
CLICK.

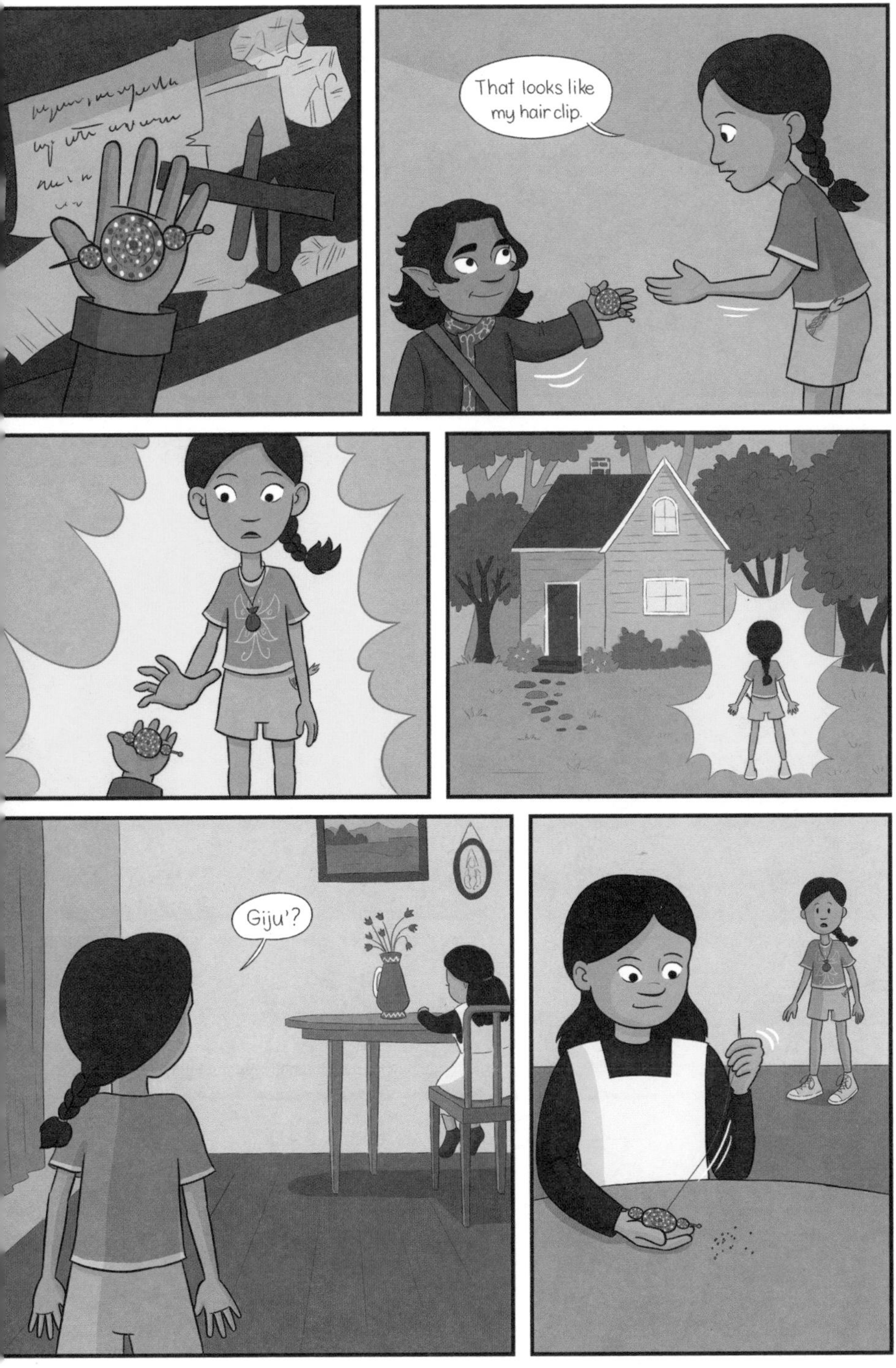
That looks like my hair clip.
Giju'?

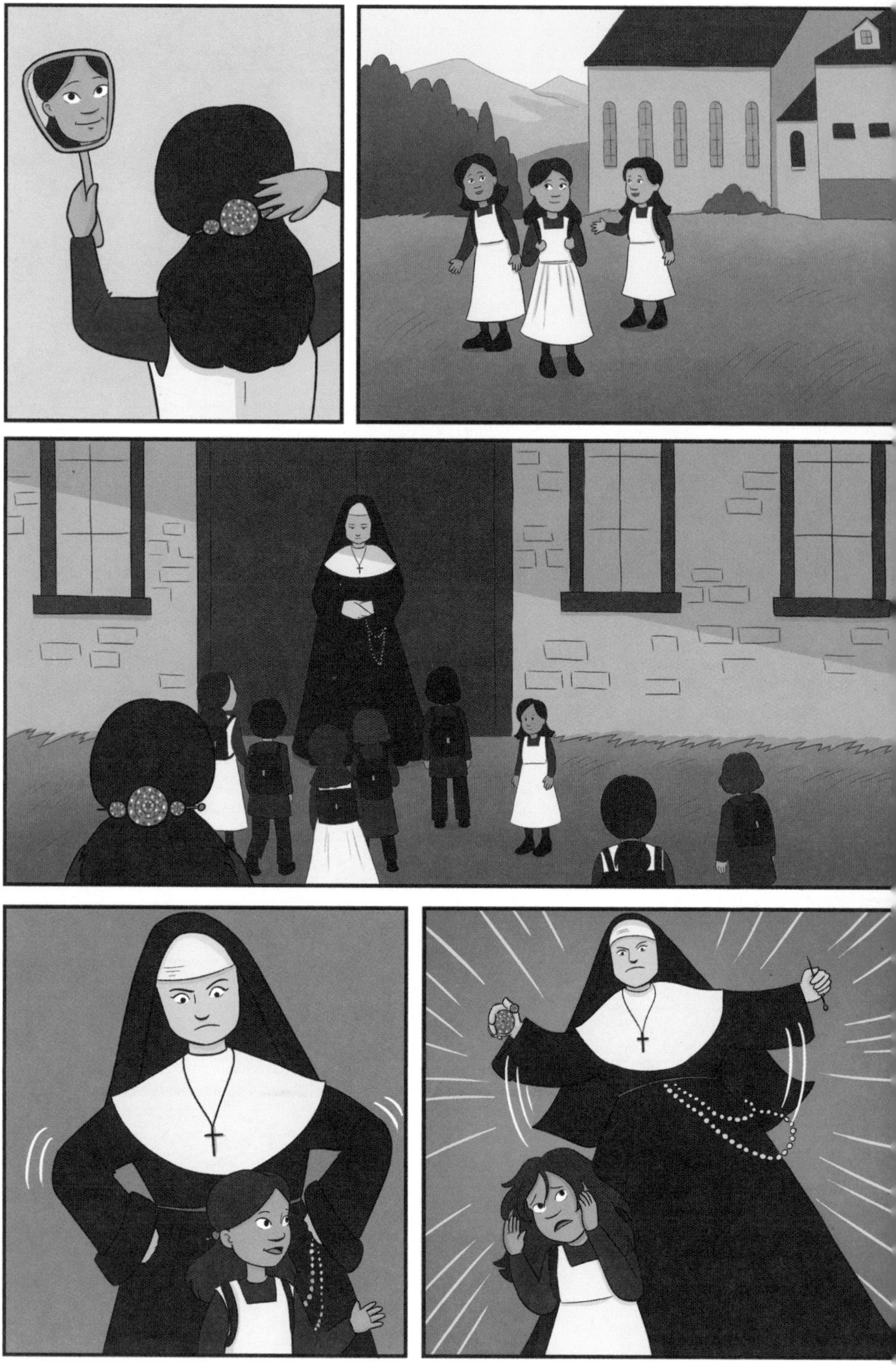

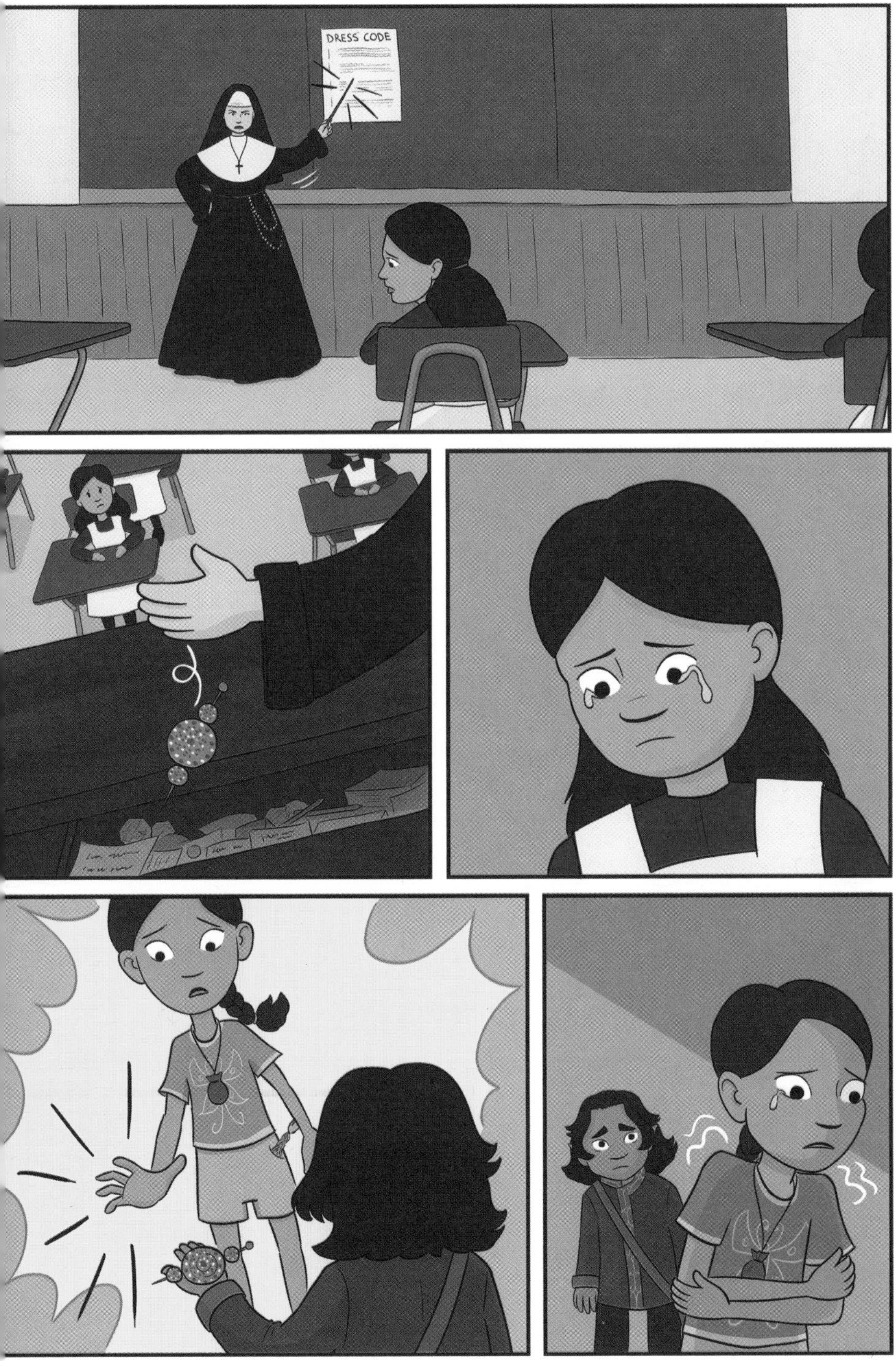
DRESS CODE

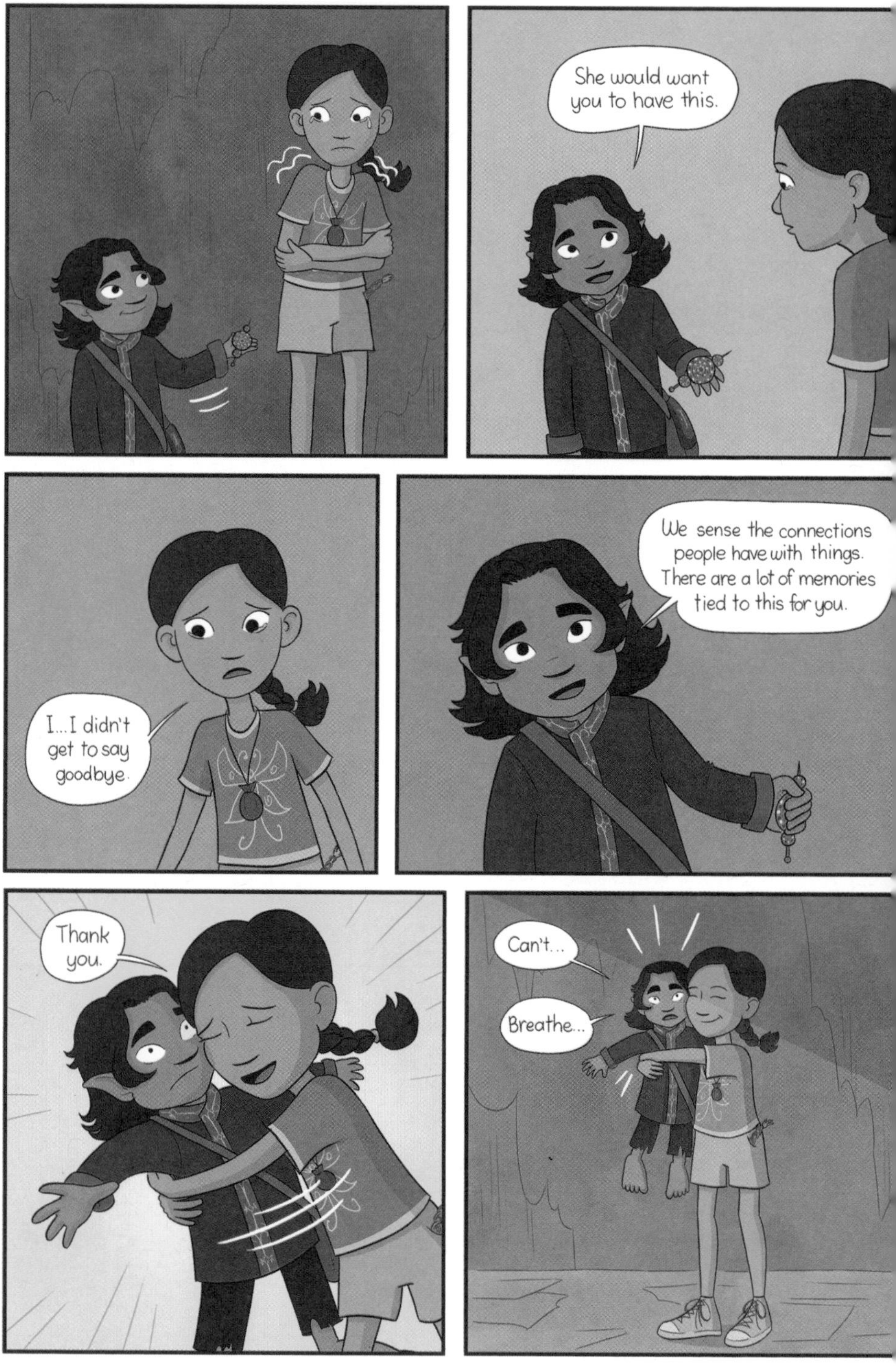
She would want you to have this.
I...I didn't get to say goodbye.
We sense the connections people have with things. There are a lot of memories tied to this for you.
Thank you.
Can't...
Breathe...

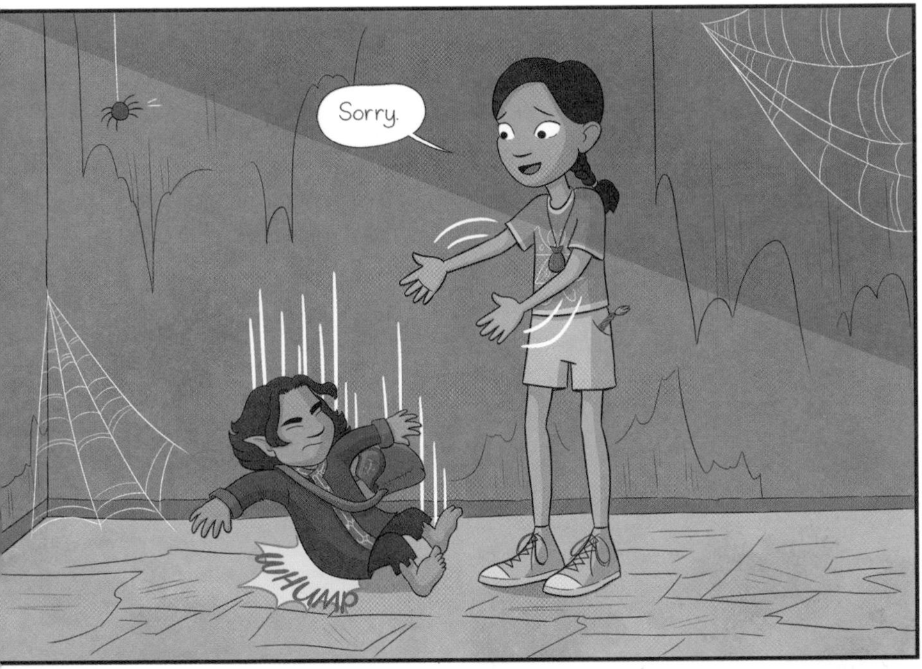
Sorry.
WHUMP

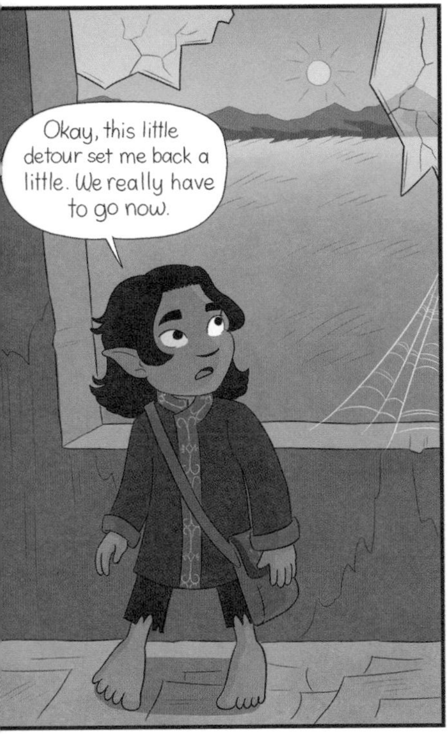
Okay, this little detour set me back a little. We really have to go now.

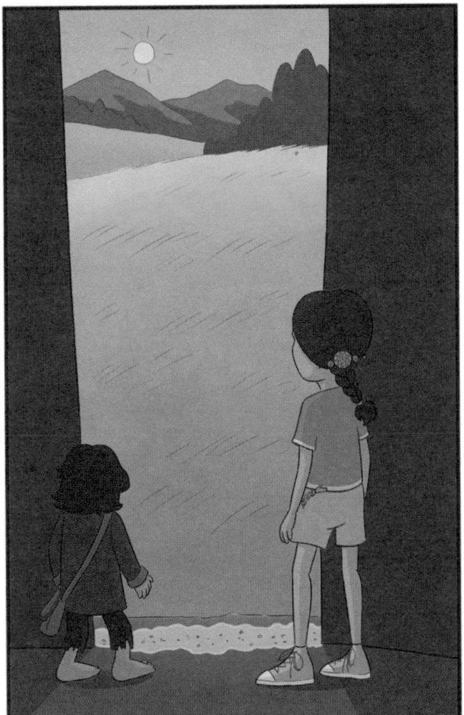

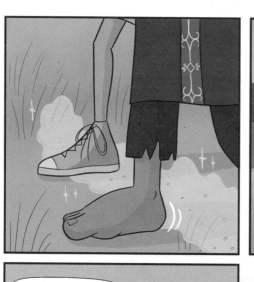

Alrighty, all we need to do now is--

PUUG!!

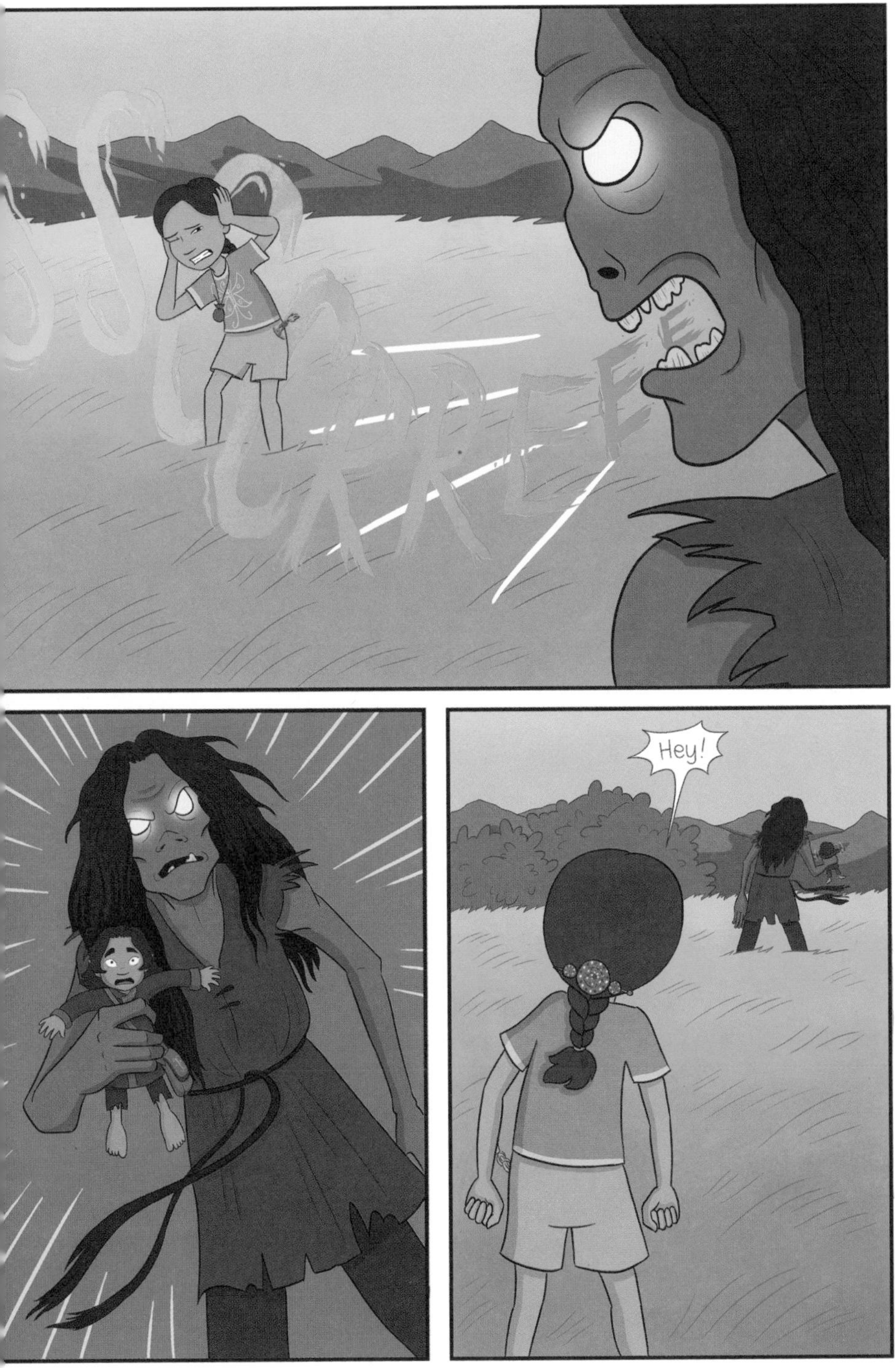
Hey!

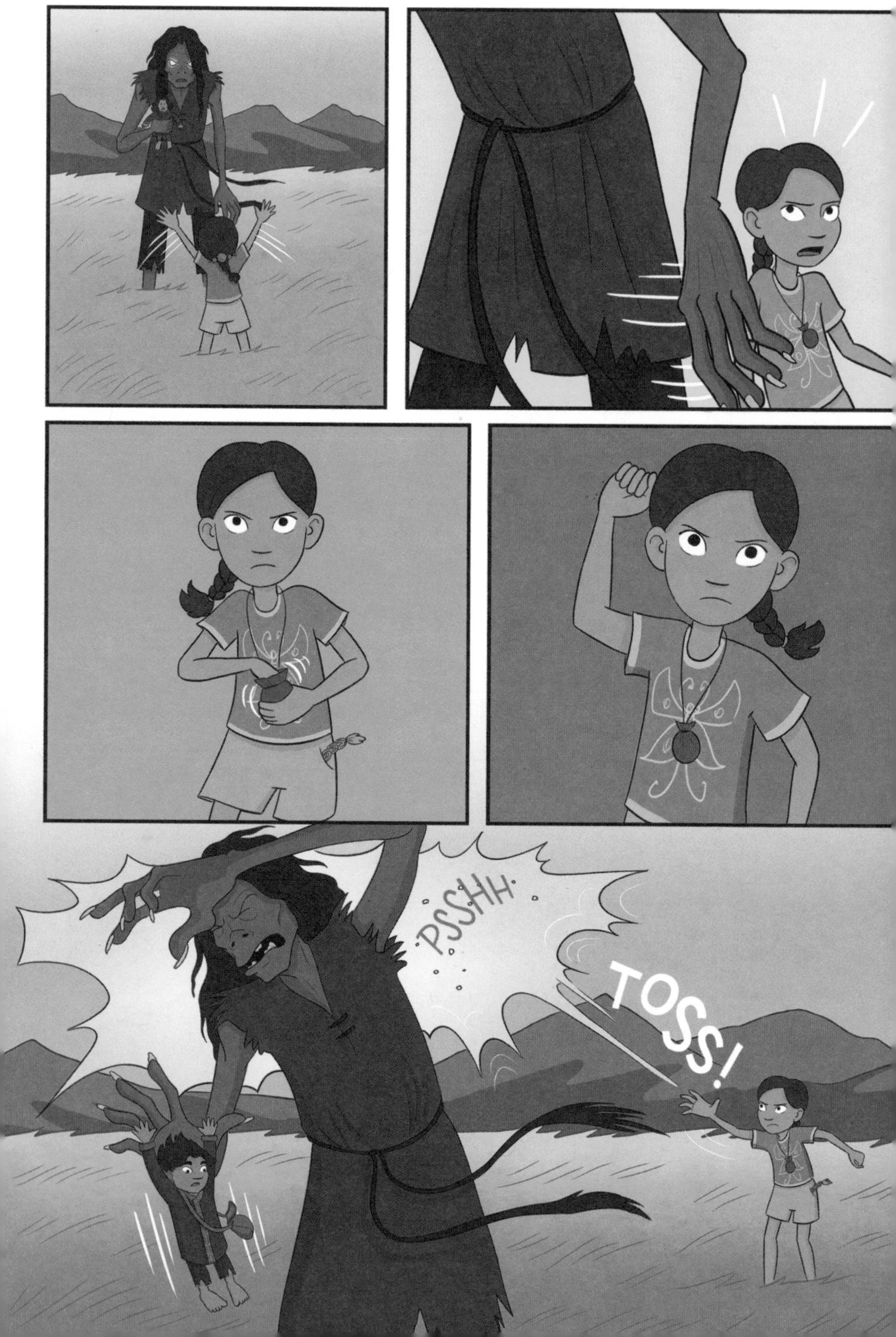
PSSHH
TOSS!

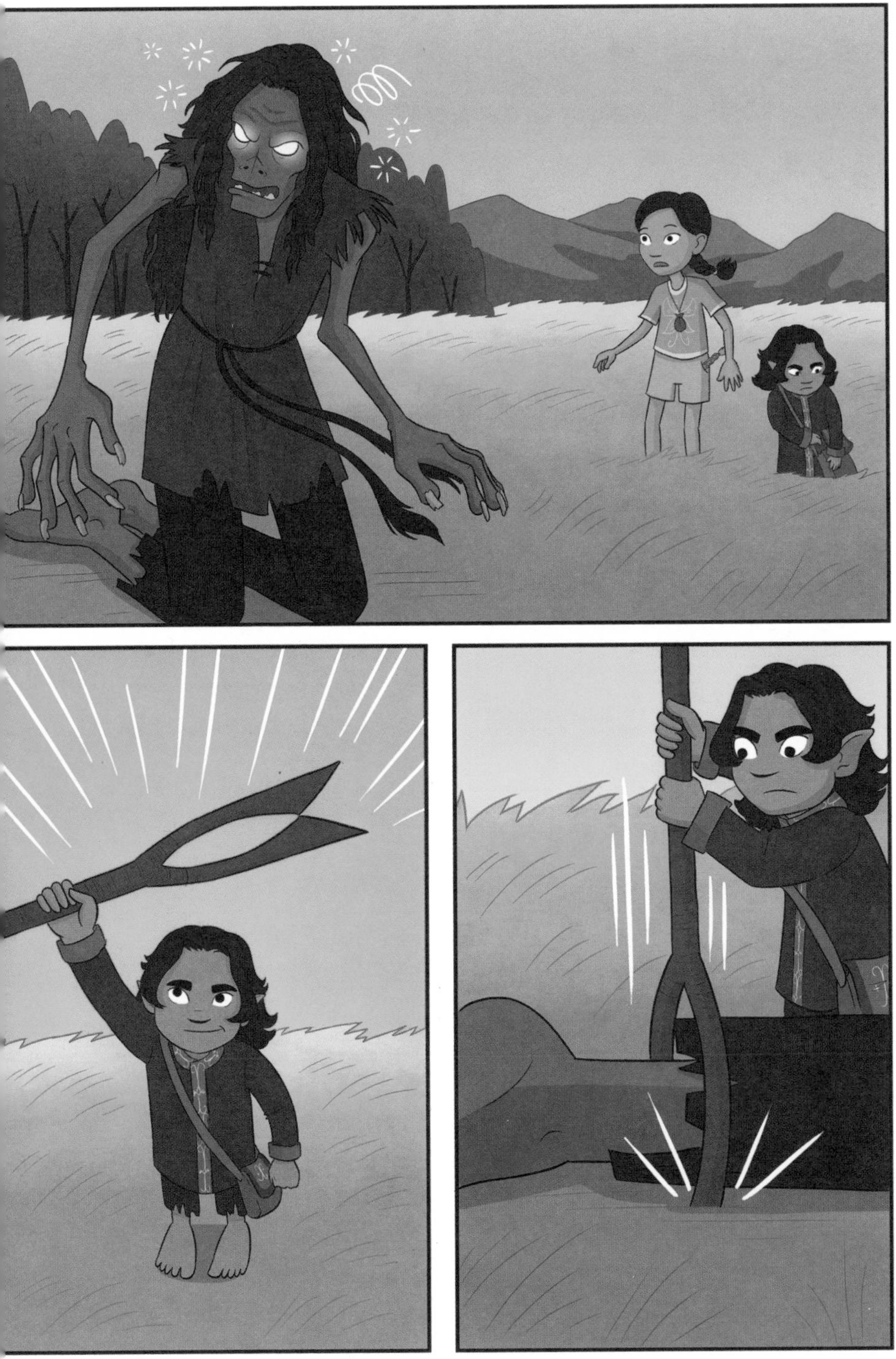

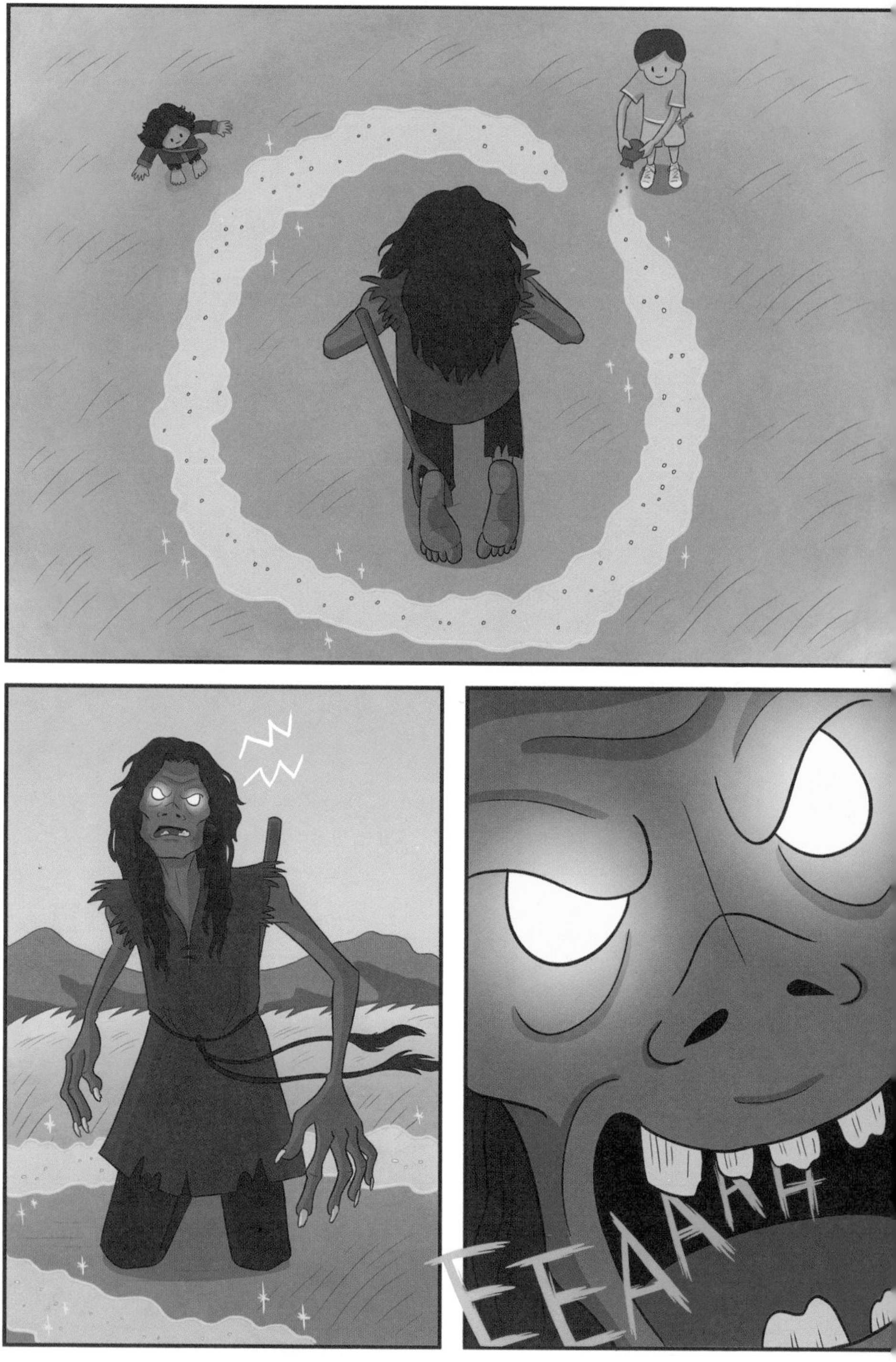
EEAAAHH

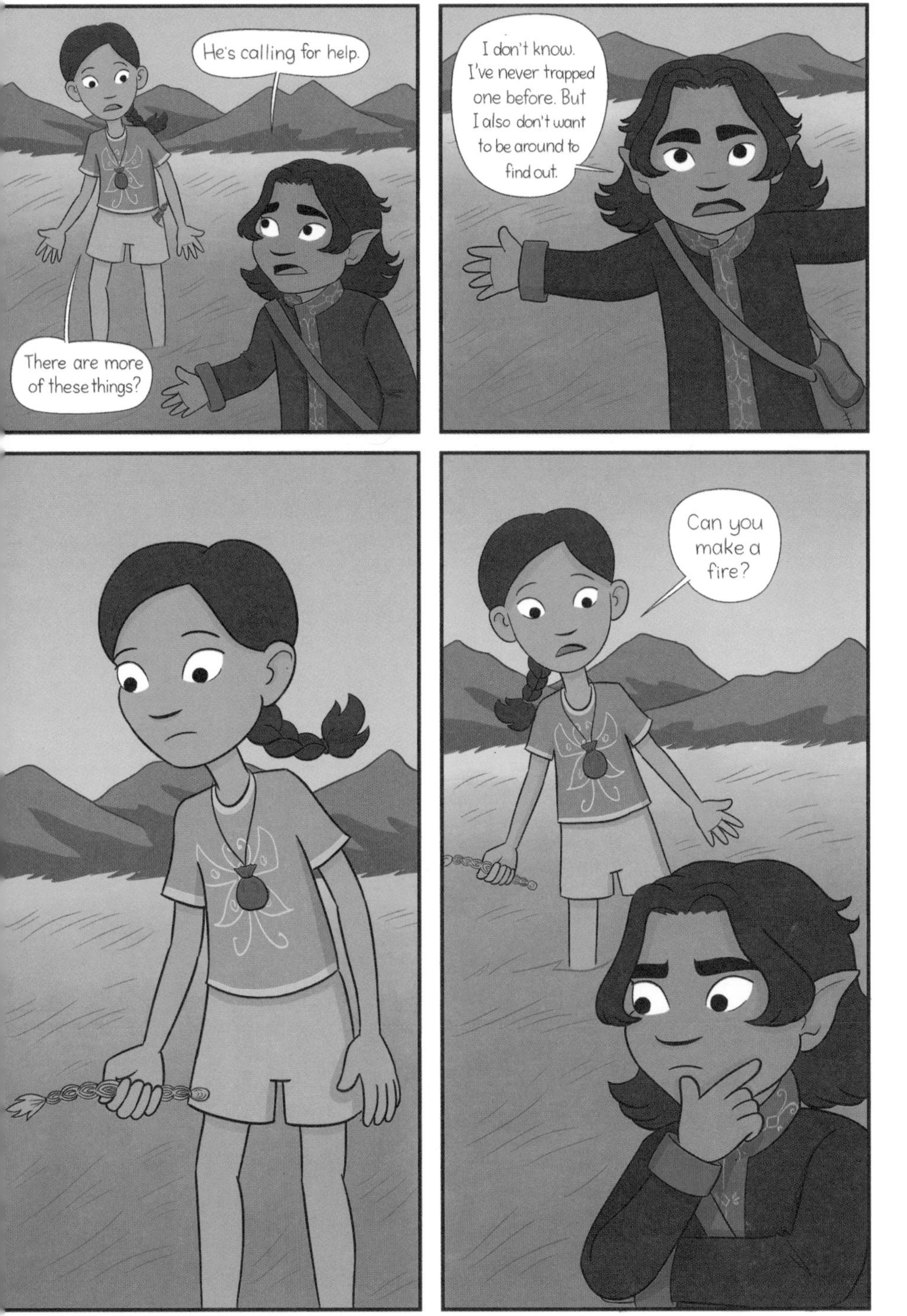
He's calling for help.
There are more of these things?
I don't know. I've never trapped one before. But I also don't want to be around to find out.
Can you make a fire?

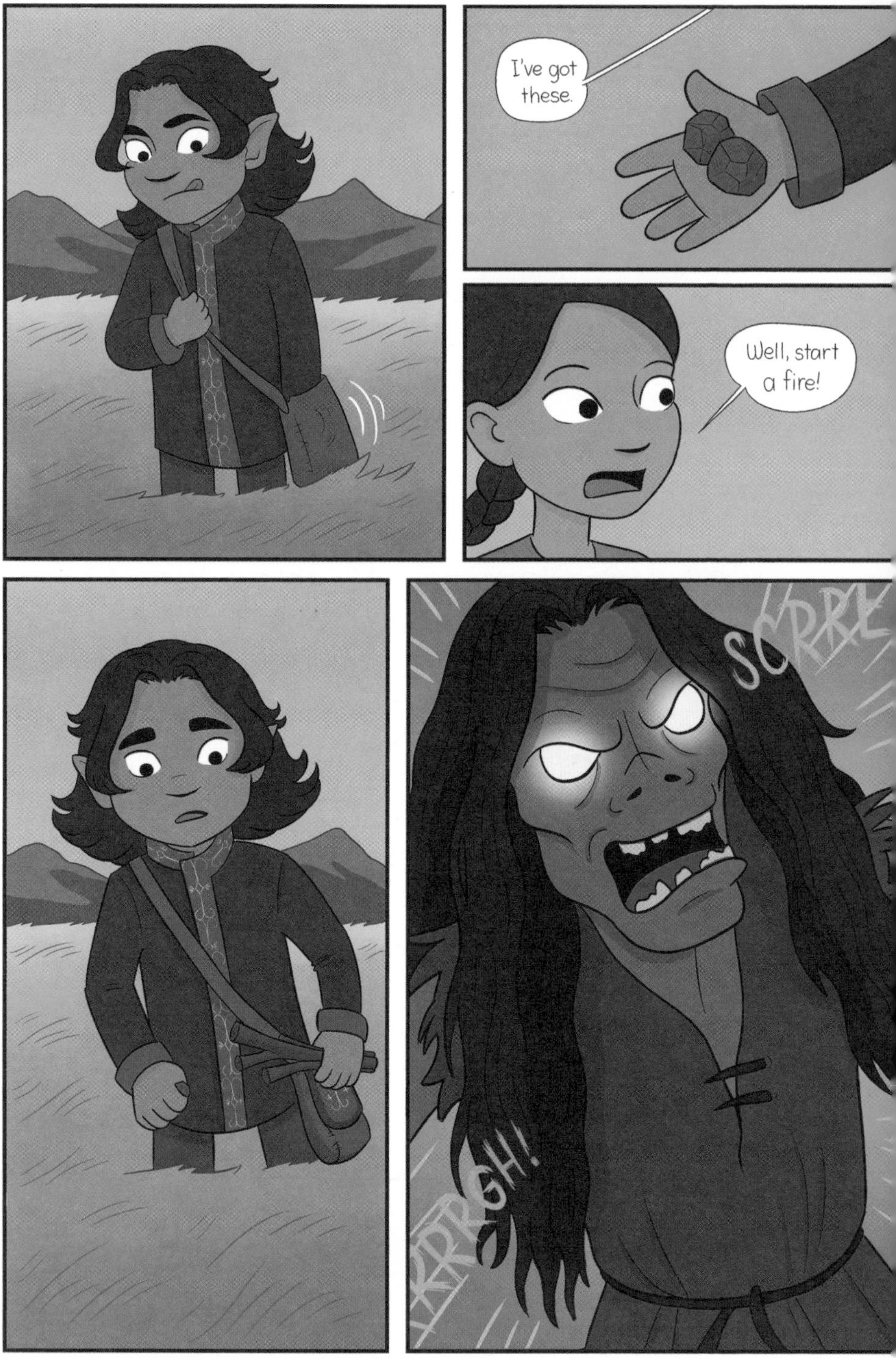
I've got these.
Well, start a fire!
SCRRE
RRRGH!

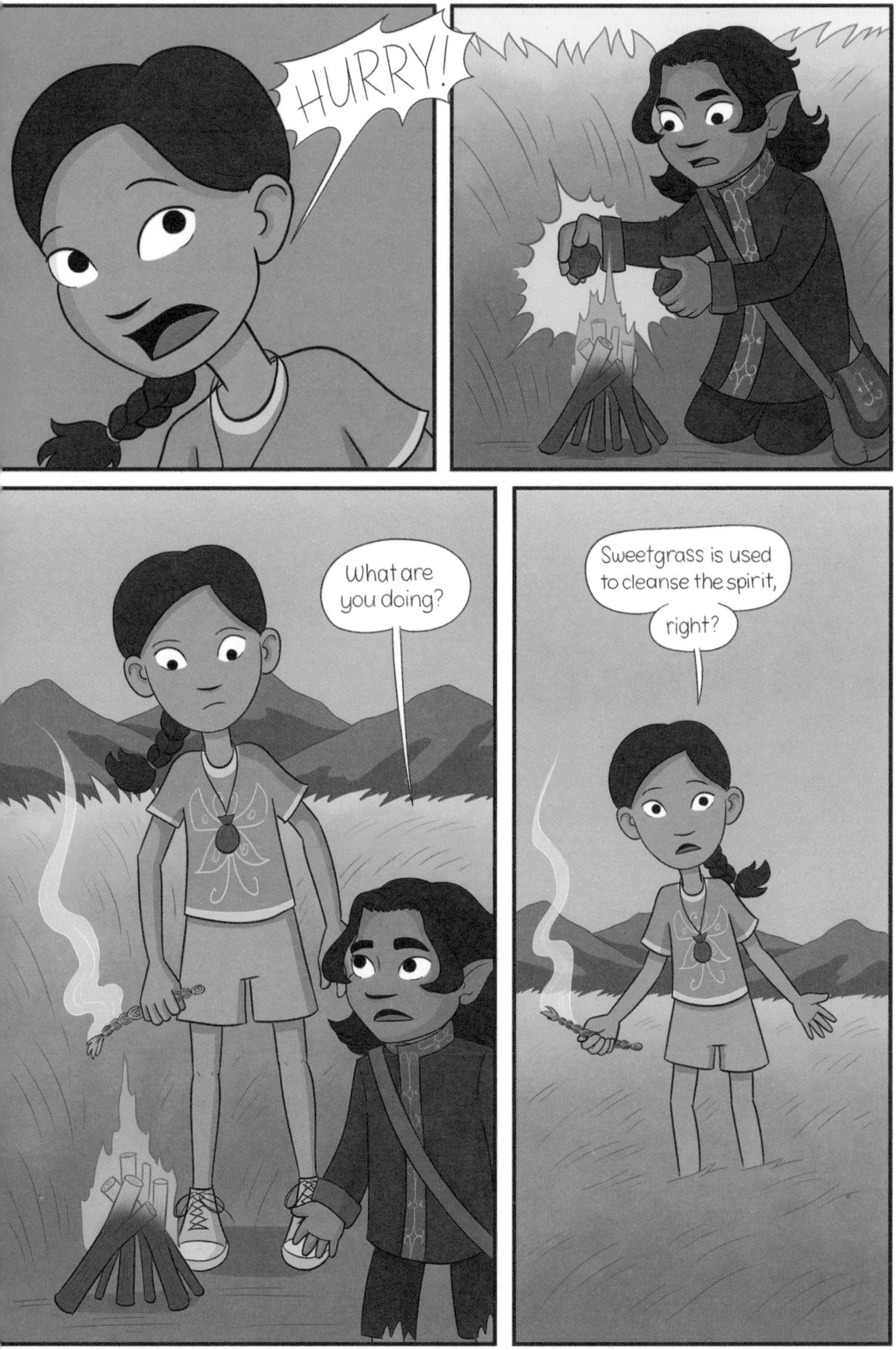
HURRY!
What are you doing?
Sweetgrass is used to cleanse the spirit,
right?

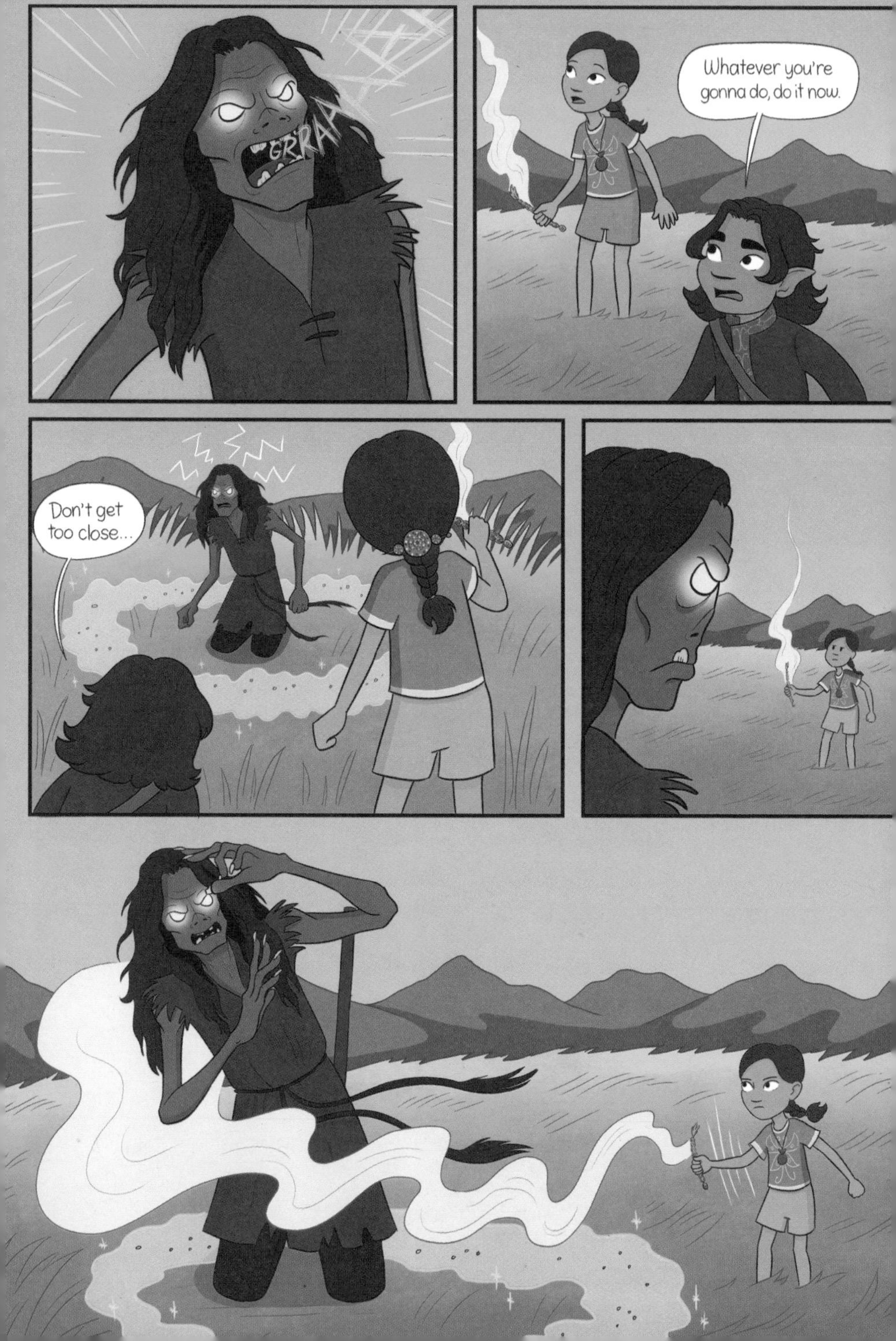
GRRAA
Whatever you're gonna do, do it now.
Don't get too close...

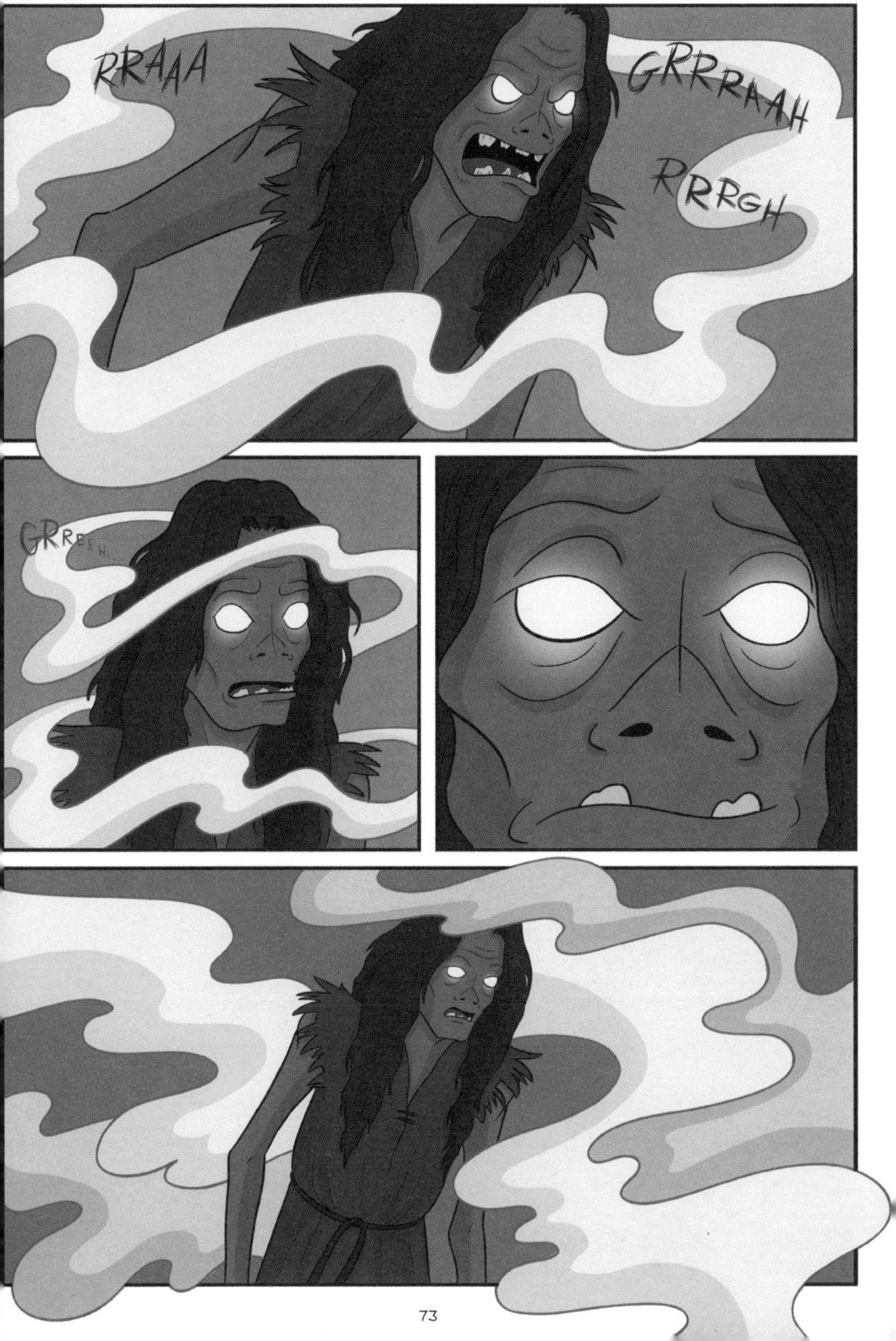
RRAAA
GRRRRAAH
RRRGH
GRREEH...

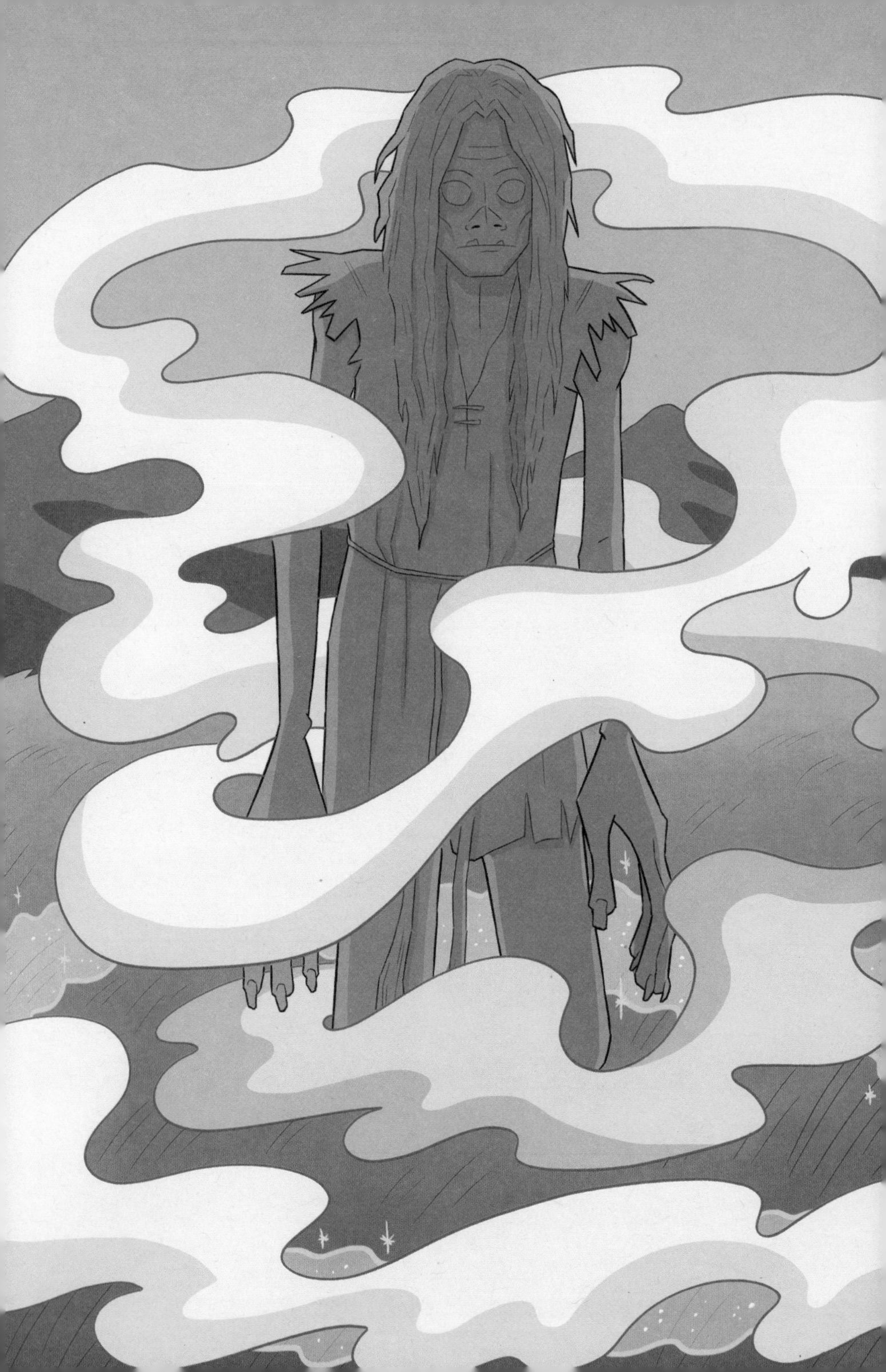

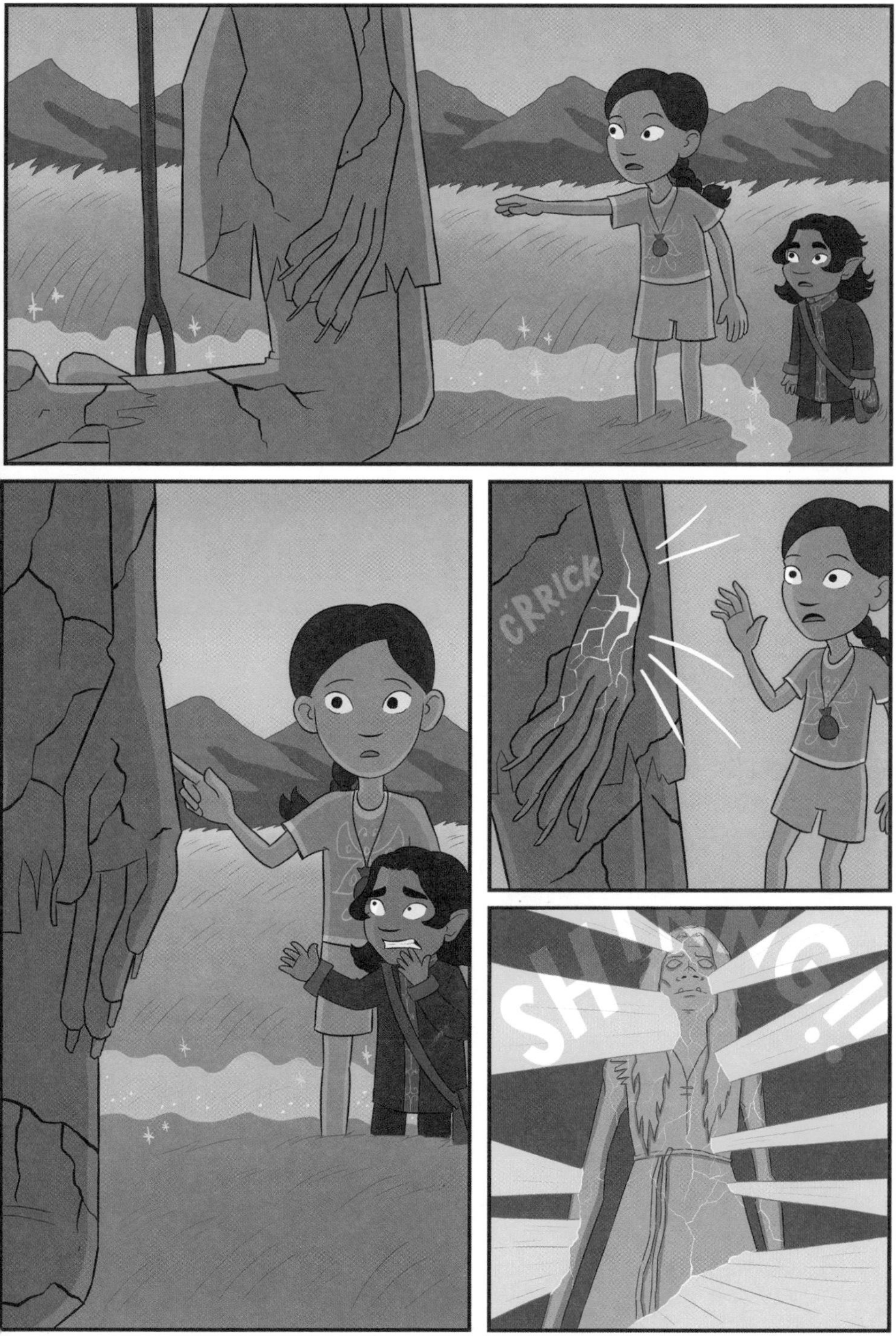
CRRICK

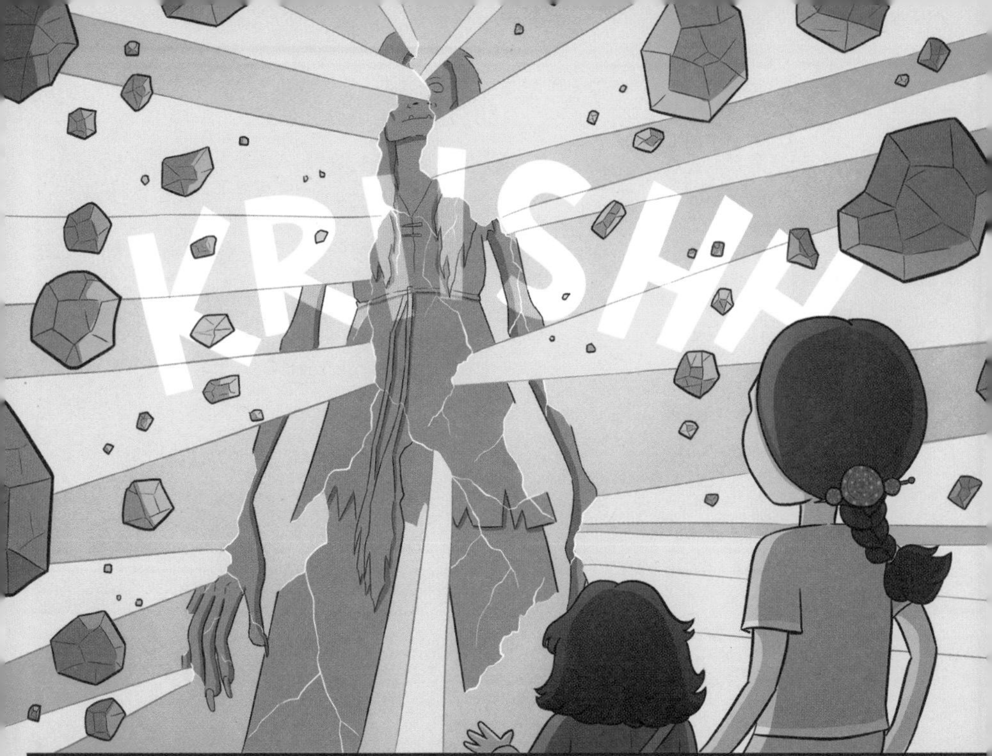
KRUSHH

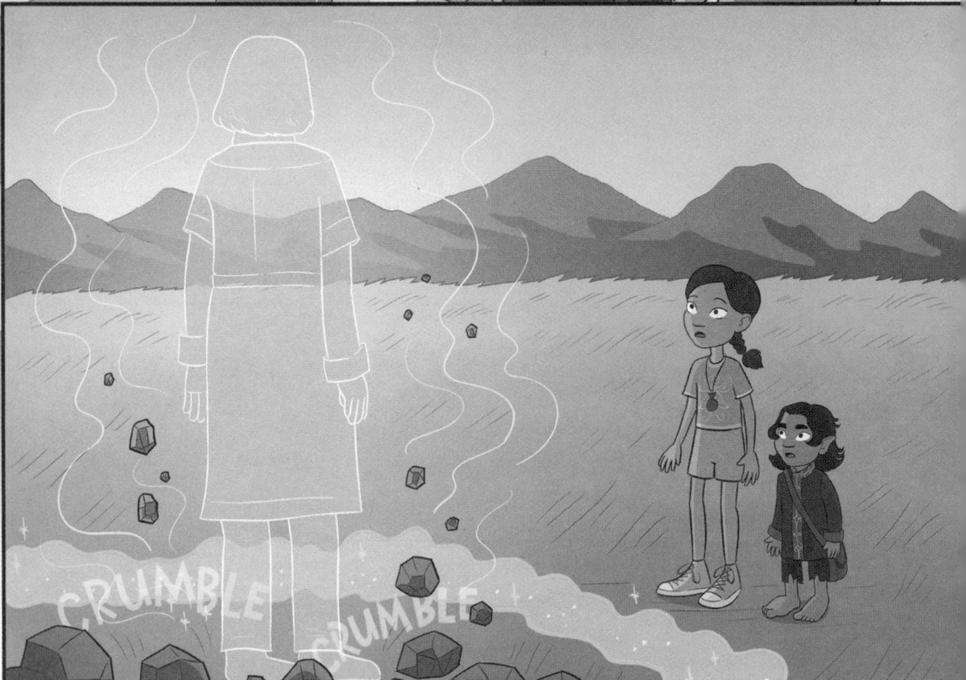
CRUMBLE
CRUMBLE

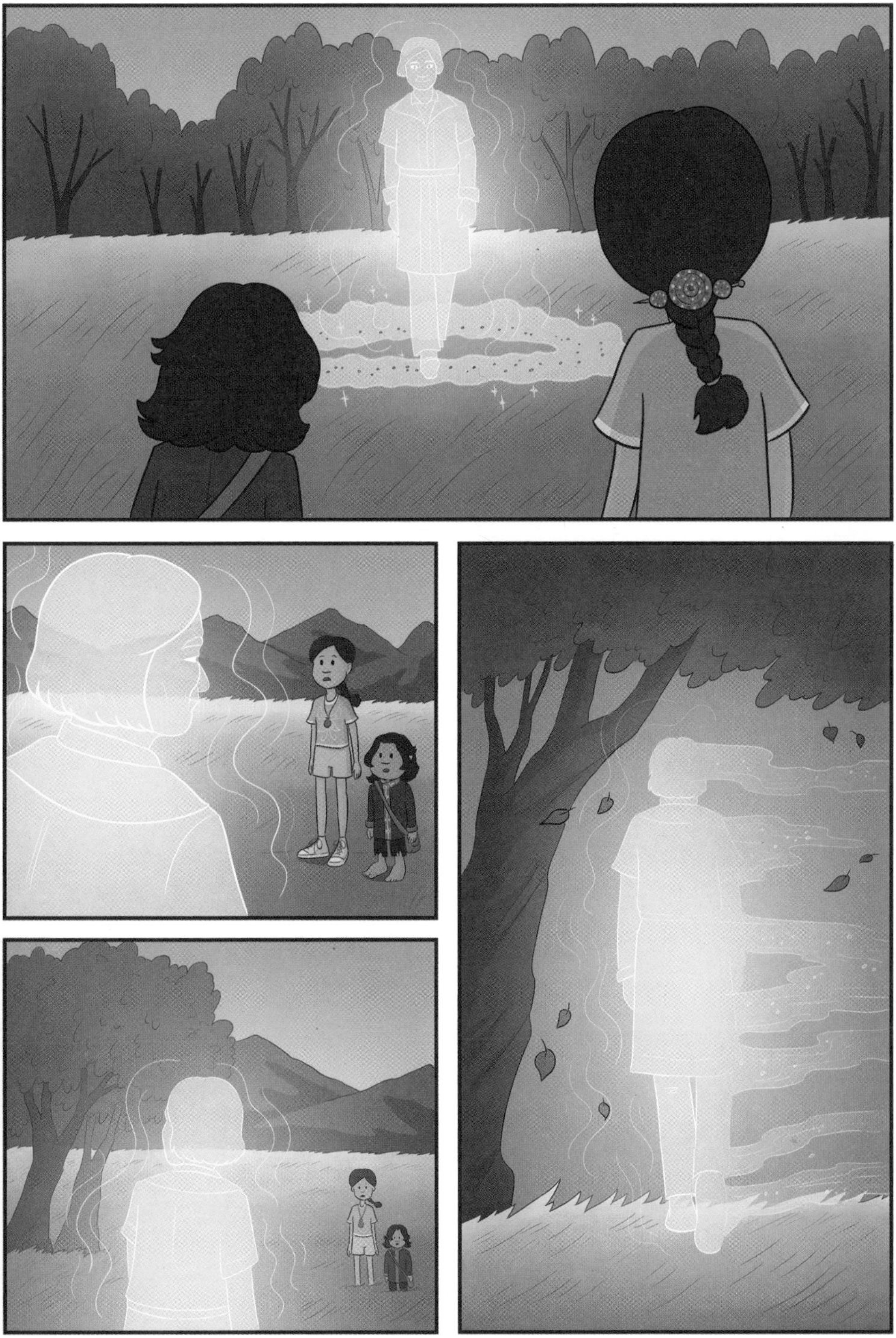

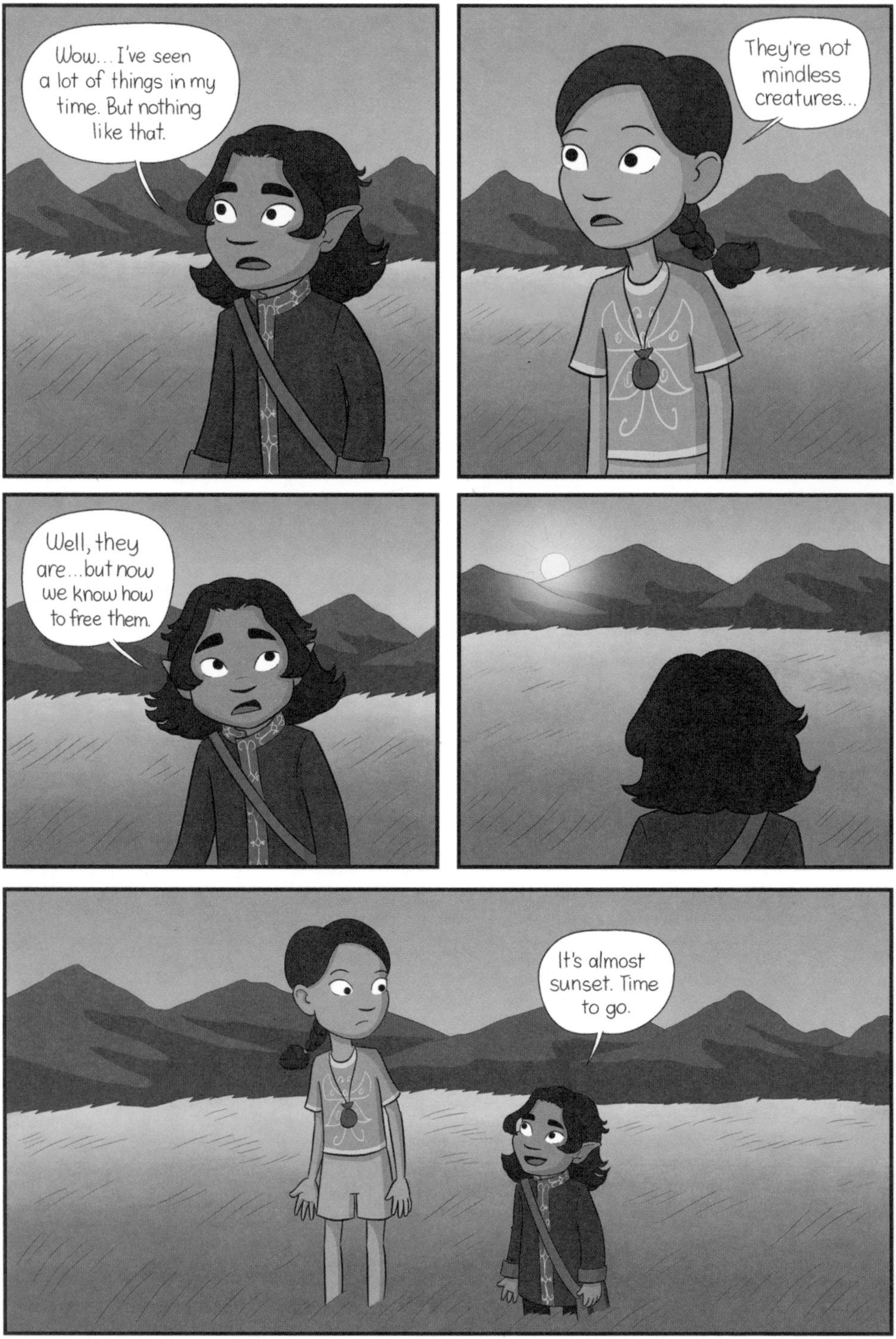
Wow... I've seen a lot of things in my time. But nothing like that.
They're not mindless creatures...
Well, they are...but now we know how to free them.
It's almost sunset. Time to go.

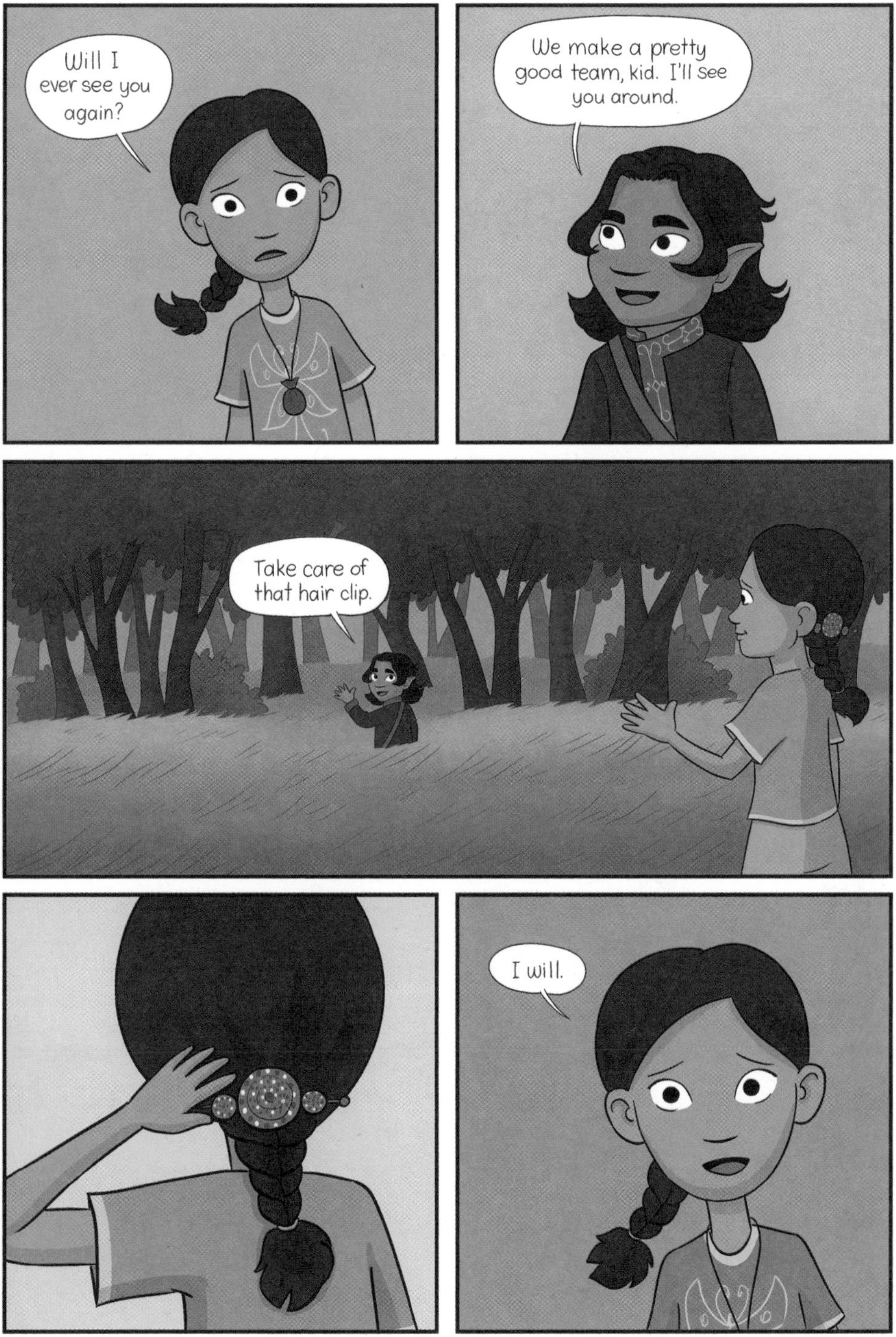
Will I ever see you again?
We make a pretty good team, kid. I'll see you around.
Take care of that hair clip.
I will.

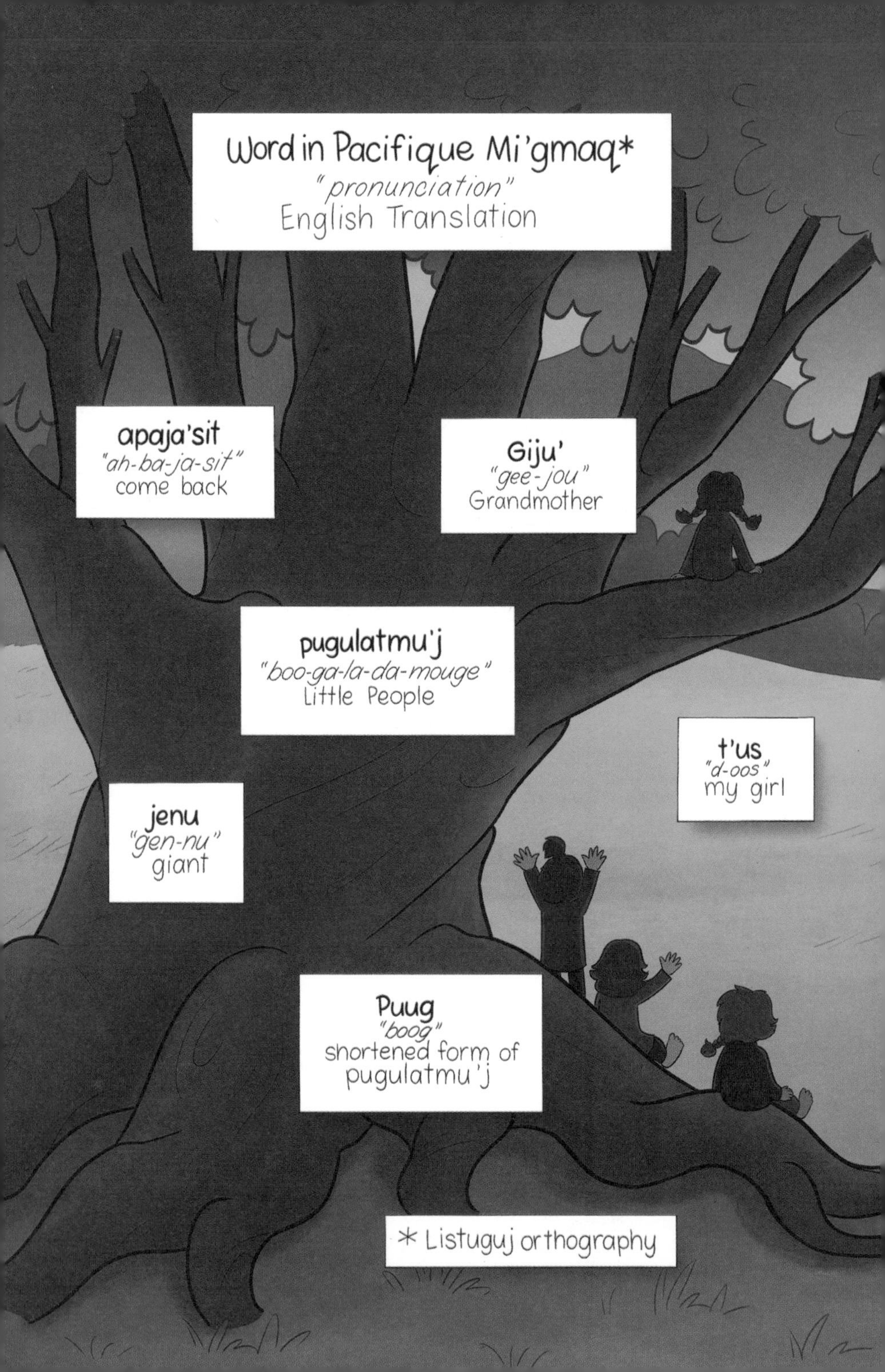

Word in Pacifique Mi'gmaq*
"pronunciation"
English Translation

apaja'sit
"ah-ba-ja-sit"
come back

Giju'
"gee-jou"
Grandmother

pugulatmu'j
"boo-ga-la-da-mouge"
Little People

t'us
"d-oos"
my girl

jenu
"gen-nu"
giant

Puug
"boog"
shortened form of pugulatmu'j

* Listuguj orthography

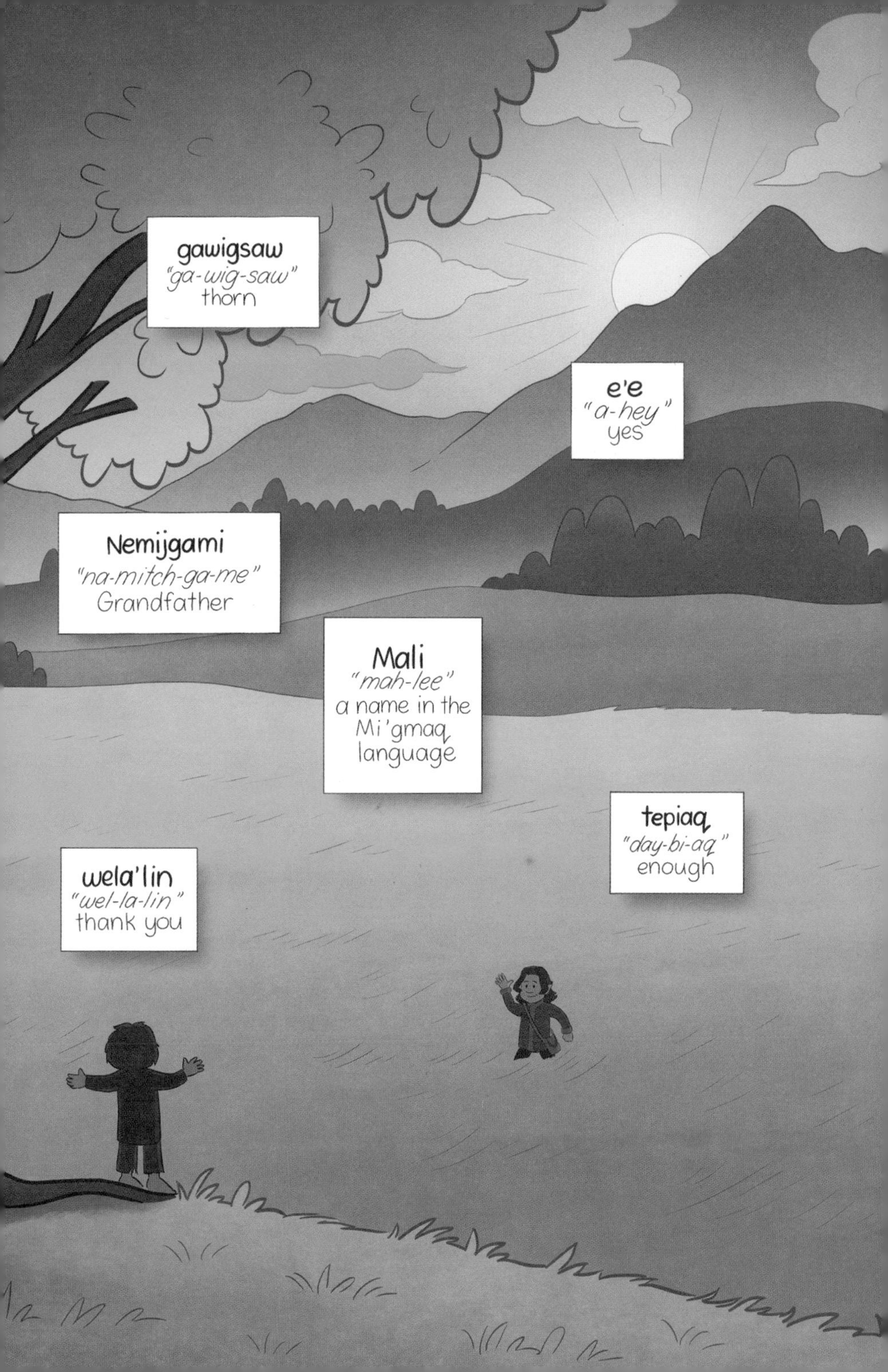
gawigsaw
"ga-wig-saw"
thorn
e'e
"a-hey"
yes
Nemijgami
"na-mitch-ga-me"
Grandfather
Mali
"mah-lee"
a name in the Mi'gmaq language
tepiaq
"day-bi-aq"
enough
wela'lin
"wel-la-lin"
thank you

 From Listuguj, Quebec, **BRANDON MITCHELL** is the founder of Birch Bark Comics and creator of the Sacred Circles comic series, which draws on his Mi'kmaq heritage. He has written five books with the Healthy Aboriginal Network (*Lost Innocence*, *Drawing Hope*, *River Run*, *Making It Right*, and *Emily's Choice*). Brandon has written and illustrated *Jean-Paul's Daring Adventure: Stories from Old Mobile* for the University of Alabama, as well as two Mi'qmaq language-based stories for the Listuguj Education Directorate. He has also completed an art installation for Heritage and Culture New Brunswick. Brandon currently resides in Fredericton, New Brunswick. @writerbrandonmitchell

 **VERONIKA BARINOVA** is an emerging illustrator currently living in Calgary. She has a Bachelor in Visual Communication Design from the Alberta University of the Arts, and works primarily in digital media. Born in Moscow, Russia, Veronika is inspired by the 90s, occult fiction, and Slavic folk tales. Her work focuses on creating engaging characters and immersive worlds for readers, and her stories often have mystical or supernatural themes with a comedic undertone. Her previous work appeared in the animated film *Buddy's Buddy*, for which she worked as a background artist.

KEEPING STORIES ALIVE:
MAKE YOUR OWN MEMORY BOX

We all have special items that hold meaning for us. These items carry our memories and stories. Create a memory box to hold these special things and keep them safe!

WHAT YOU'LL NEED

- small cardboard box such as a shoebox
- art supplies such as stickers, markers, or paints
- index cards or a small notebook to record stories and memories
- small objects that hold special meaning for you

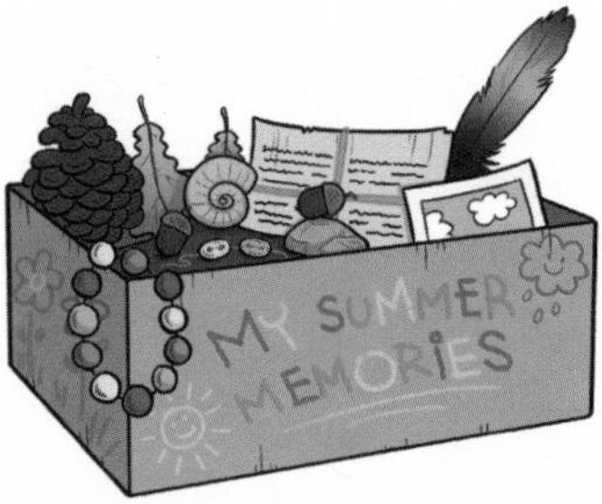
MY SUMMER MEMORIES

HOW TO MAKE A MEMORY BOX

1. Decorate the box using stickers, markers, paints, or other art supplies. Make it your own. Be creative and have fun!

2. Give your memory box a special name. Write the name on the box, like "My Summer Memories" or "Grade Three."

3. With help from an adult, find items you want to keep safe in your memory box. Find objects that hold special meaning to you. These objects might include favourite photos, drawings, or letters. Remember these items are important to you, so hold onto them carefully.

4. Write a short memory or story for each item.

5. Keep your memory box in a safe place. Visit your memory box when you're feeling happy. Or visit your memory box when you're feeling sad and need help cheering up. Share your memories with friends and family.

ADVENTURES OF THE PUGULATMU'J

In this series of graphic novels for young readers, a Mi'kmaw girl goes on adventures and meets figures inspired by traditional stories.

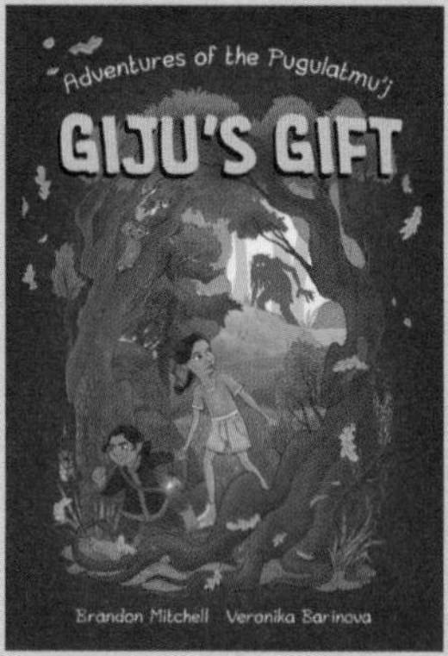
Adventures of the Pugulatmu'j
GIJU'S GIFT
Brandon Mitchell Veronika Barinova

VOLUME 1:
GIJU'S GIFT

VOLUME 2:
IN SEARCH OF GLOOSCAP
(COMING SOON!)

FIND OUT MORE

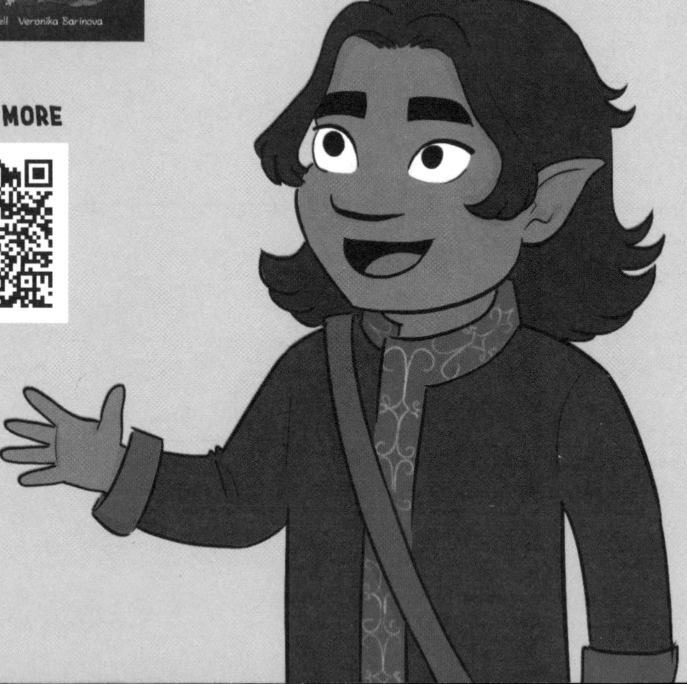